In the spirit of the holiday and a wish for familial harmony, Irene Adler persuades her detective husband to invite his brother Mycroft to Christmas luncheon. Holmes had cut ties with his brother when he discovered the machinations Mycroft employed that drove Sherlock and Adler apart for four years. He isn't really sure this reunion is a great idea, but he can deny his wife nothing.

Of course, they can't tell the children what Mycroft is to them, as that would entail learning that their father is the celebrated detective when they know him simply as Lucca Sapori. And just when they think things may be going better than expected, ghosts of the past crop up in unexpected ways and threaten to ruin the holidays for everyone.

Christmas at the Sapori's
Copyright © 2022 K D Sherrinford
ISBN: 978-1-4874-3684-1
Cover art by Martine Jardin

Published by eXtasy Books Inc

Look for us online at:
www.eXtasybooks.com

# CHRISTMAS AT THE SAPORI'S SHERLOCK HOLMES AND IRENE ADLER MYSTERIES 2

## BY

## K D SHERRINFORD

# DEDICATION

*To my late farther Denis O'Doherty*


# ACKNOWLEDGEMENTS

This book has been inspired by the works of Sir Arthur Conan Doyle, featuring characters recognisable from his original stories.

I would like to thank my family and friends for their kindness and inspirational thoughts. My husband John for his patience and understanding. My wonderful children David & Katie for always believing in me. My sister Lesley, my sister-in-law Christine, and my niece Caroline for not writing me off as completely mad.

This book would never have been completed without the help and support of the following people.

Abigail McIntosh, for her extraordinary vision, support and guidance.

For my golden girls, Jayne Leahy and Gayna Dagnall for their unwavering assistance, and for making this such a special journey.

I am for ever grateful to my team of Beta-readers for their insightful suggestions.

The amazing publishing team at Extasy Books. The Editor in Chief Jay Austin for her never-ending patience, and Martine Jardin for her stunning covers.

Lastly, to you the readers — an enormous thank you.

# Introduction: Irene (Nene) Adler

Our ever-growing capacity for love and acceptance is unceasingly complex, for no one can give us the love we desire in precisely the way we want, no more than we can offer those we love the same thing.

Success in any relationship is defined by our willingness to endure despite the challenges we encounter along the way. Finding happiness had taken me a while and involved a rather strange journey, but I was finally with the man I loved. Perhaps not in the conventional sense, but in all the ways that mattered.

When Sherlock Holmes and I finally reconciled in 1899, our joy at being together again was inexpressible. But our happiness carried a significant encumbrance, for we had a child to consider. We agreed it would be impossible to take our son to England and live together as man and wife. Thanks to Colonel Moriarty, we would face a furore from the London underworld if they ever suspected we were back together.

We had a right to live in peace, not fear for our lives. So Sherlock took over the identity of Lucca Sapori, the brother-in-law of our close friend Violetta Esporito, and my husband and I married again at the all'anagrafe — the registry office in Milan — re-affirming our love as Mr and Mrs Sapori.

Lucca Sapori was a former intelligence officer in the Royal Italian Navy who disappeared in 1894 following the tragic death of his wife, Arianne (Violetta's sister). Violetta and her daughter Ava asked Holmes to try and track Sapori down and, with Mycroft's assistance, they eventually found him.

Sapori had emigrated to Canada under the assumed name of Sergio Regio, where he fell in love with and married an heiress from Toronto. Sapori wrote to Mycroft explaining that he was happy in his new life and had no plans to return to Italy.

Before Sherlock and I reunited, he and his brother devised a plan for him to take over Sapori's identity. First they asked Violetta's permission—she was happy to give it. After that, Mycroft arranged for forged documents, even creating a bogus position for Sapori at the cabinet office on Great Smith Street where Mycroft was employed and utterly indispensable to the British Government. As my husband said, his brother *was* the British Government.

After our honeymoon in Paris, Sherlock returned to Baker Street to continue his occupation as the world's greatest consulting detective. He remained firmly devoted to his career and his family in equal measure. This was an elaborate deception, which few were aware of. Still, the underworld no longer associated Sherlock Holmes with Irene Adler. My husband thought it wonderfully ironic to be impersonating a man who was already impersonating another.

Since our marriage, Sherlock and I had worked constantly, sometimes on different continents. But we travelled to see each other whenever possible, often in disguise. Because we spent so much time apart, we never grew tired of one another. Holmes joked that if he were with me all the time, I would likely have killed him by now. He said he would then return as a ghost to investigate his murder. I wouldn't put it past him.

Still, apart from caring for our son Nicco, I lived my life above and beyond that of a dutiful wife, finding solace in my charity work, my occupation as a contralto at La Scala, and teaching at the theatre school.

My husband and I learned that to succeed in a long-distance relationship one had to acquiesce, which was a learning process. So I was content in my marriage. Sherlock was a good husband and a considerate and attentive lover during our time together.

One of the most memorable times we spent together as a family was the Christmas of 1904 at our second home, Ash Tree Farm, on the beautiful Sussex Downs. What I was hoping to be a perfect family Christmas turned out to be a time full of deception, drama, and intrigue, which laid a few ghosts to rest along the way. The following is an account of that time.

# CHAPTER ONE: FAMILY LIFE

M y husband only took on the alias of Lucca Sapori in the
first place because of one man — Colonel James Moriarty, the brother of the infamous Professor Moriarty. The man
who fell to his death at the Reichenbach falls after an abortive
attempt to murder his nemesis, Sherlock Holmes.

Colonel Moriarty suffered a breakdown shortly after learning of his brother's demise and was subsequently committed
to the Bedlam insane asylum. However, with the assistance of
Wild Bill Palmer and the Tooley Street Gang, Colonel Moriarty was sprung from the asylum three years later upon discovering Sherlock Holmes had returned to London.

Moriarty followed Sherlock and me to Fiesole. He warned
us that our lives would be in grave danger if we returned to
London and the underworld discovered we were together.
Ironically, thanks to Colonel Moriarty and our adventures in
Fiesole, Sherlock and I finally became parents to our amazing
son Nicco. But it was our beautiful daughter Charlotte who
completed our family.

On an April night four and a half years earlier, she was
born at our home in Milan.

Holmes took his responsibilities as a father seriously. The
depths of loyalty that existed in his extraordinary brain man-
ifested themselves in a deep abiding love and our close family
bond. The children adored their father. Sherlock was firm but
fair. He always took an avid interest in everything they did,
always curious to hear what they had learned each day.

Now soon to be nine, Nicco was just like his father —

1

fiercely intelligent, serious, and intellectual. Highly motivated and self-disciplined from an early age, Nicco was never anything less than the top of his class. At the same time, Charlotte took after me—intelligent, stubborn, dramatic, always getting into scrapes, and usually aided and abetted by our rescued family dog, Helen. Despite Charlotte's tender years, beneath that engaging smile lay a rebellious streak that Sherlock described as a force of nature.

Charlotte was an enigma in many ways. She learned to read and had an extensive vocabulary by the time she was two years old, perfectly happy explaining how no two leaves on any single tree are identical and then, in the next breath, refusing to eat her vegetables or requiring help to tie her shoelaces.

When Charlotte watched Nicco and her father play chess at age three, she was utterly fascinated by how the pieces moved around the board. Nicco patiently taught her to play until she memorised every move. Charlotte beat her brother for the first time when she was four, which was no mean feat, as Nicco was an accomplished player. However, despite Charlotte's best efforts, she could never beat her father Sherlock.

# CHAPTER TWO: ASH TREE FARM

Sherlock and I purchased Ash Tree farm, located just outside Amberley on the beautiful Sussex Downs, in the spring of that year. The farm required extensive renovation, but we immediately fell in love with its rustic charm, the hills' breathtaking views, and the rolling chalk grassland overlooking the River Arun.

Sherlock ordered the workers to carry out extensive repairs, including fence replacements for the ten acres of paddocks and fields and a new roof to the stable block. The main farmhouse benefitted from a refurbished kitchen, upgraded bathrooms, and replacement wooden flooring.

I came over from Milan in the summer to see how the renovations were going. I was excited at the prospect of spending our first Christmas there as a family on my husband's home turf. With the renovations underway, Sherlock and I stayed at the Three Tunnes Inn, which was situated a mile from the farm. However, my husband had converted the shed at the bottom of the farmhouse garden into a den. One sunny afternoon, he took great delight in showing the den to me. Afterwards we walked around the fields and talked to the labourers replacing the fencing.

I had never seen Sherlock look so energised and alive as he spoke of his plans for the farm, showing me his outlines.

"Well, what do you think?" He gestured to the inside of the shed, which looked rather cosy with its taper candles, small table and chairs, and a comfortable-looking bed in the corner.

"It looks better than I first imagined," I admitted. "But it's still a shed. Why would you sleep here when you have a comfortable room at the Inn?"

"Because I like to supervise the labourers. There's a lot to be done before Christmas, and I cannot always be here. I have to get back to Baker Street." Sherlock sat on the bed and took my hand. "Sit with me." He fixed me with a gaze of keen penetration, one with which I was so familiar.

"I know that look. You must be insane if you think I'm staying here with you tonight. Have you forgotten? You promised me dinner at the Royal Oak."

"Yes, of course." His eyes crinkled. "Very well, if that's what you want. Although I *did* organise a picnic for our convenience." He pointed to a large wicker basket sitting in the corner. "We have game pie, ham, wine, bread, and cheese. What more could we need?" He laughed, cupping my face with his hands and gazing into my eyes. "Where's your sense of adventure? What happened to that girl in Fiesole who offered to live in a cave with me?"

"She would have back then, in a heartbeat."

"And now?" he quizzed, gazing at me questioningly.

"That girl's still here, but she now has two children."

"Ah, but the children are not here with us now, they are in Milan. At least take wine with me."

"Why not," I replied. "What wine do you have?" I gestured towards the basket.

"It's a Bordeaux from Château Cheval Blanc. It comes highly recommended."

"Are you toying with me, husband? If I didn't know better, I would think you were trying to lead me astray."

"Well-deduced, Nene." Sherlock laughed. "I rather think I am."

He opened the bottle and poured out two glasses then handed one to me.

"This is excellent." I sipped slowly from the glass, not once taking my focus off my husband.

His gaze was one of anticipation and expectation. I hesitated for a moment, enthralled by his eyes. Then, before I knew what he was about, he drew me in by the waist and pulled me to him. His lips brushed mine. They pressed down softly at first, becoming more urgent as his tentative fingertips stroked my face and neck.

I heard the bold, charismatic repertoire of a song thrush in the distance. The prick of the fresh hay in the field, my husband's cologne, and the thrill of his touch were intoxicating. They reminded me of our first time together in Fiesole when we made a mark on each other's souls which would stay with us forever, obsessed as anyone falling under the spell of love and all the madness that entails.

Suddenly Sherlock pulled away. He rose to his feet and reached for his cap. "Forgive me," he said. "Come, let's go back to the Inn and change for dinner."

"Well, that's a shame," I said. "The man I fell in love with would never have given up that easily."

He spun around to face me, staring at me with a burning intensity. "Well, in that case, Mrs Sapori, I would hate to disappoint you."

We never made it to the restaurant that evening.

## Chapter Three: The Invitation. Wednesday the 21st of December

"Promise you won't be upset by my suggestion," I said.

"I can't promise that. Why, what is it?" Sherlock languidly raised his eyes from his newspaper and gazed at me suspiciously.

"I think we should invite your brother for Christmas luncheon."

Sherlock's piercing grey eyes stared at me intensely. "Have you taken leave of your senses, Nene? We're barely on speaking terms after what Mycroft did."

"We have to try and forgive him for the children's sake. Mycroft is their uncle, even if they don't know it yet. Your brother wrote to me several times wishing to atone for his behaviour in Fiesole. What does that say about us if we can't forgive him?"

Sherlock nodded. "Very well, if that's what you want. Although I'm not going to pretend I'm happy about the situation. I haven't spent Christmas with my brother since we were boys, but I'll do it for you." He smiled at me, although I could sense his displeasure. My husband was no fan of Christmas. He avoided fraternising with others the way Dracula avoided the sun.

"Good, I'm glad. It's about time," I said. "Should I call Mycroft or write to him to let him know?"

"No need. I shall arrange to meet him at the Diogenes Club. I have to go to London tomorrow. I'll do it then."

"And I think it's only fair that the servants have the day off, too. Don't worry." I laughed as Sherlock rolled his eyes. "Agnes promised to set the fires on Christmas morning. Violetta sent me some recipes, and I've ordered a turkey and a joint of beef," I said grandly, displaying an air of confidence I wasn't exactly feeling. "If you can help with the horses, I'll do the rest. It's only for one day."

"All right." Sherlock conceded. "With no disrespect to your culinary skills, Nene, it is indeed fortunate Mrs Hudson offered to help."

"Duly noted. I know you are away tomorrow, but why don't we do something together the day before Christmas Eve? We could have dinner at the Royal Oak. I've hardly seen you these past few days."

"I'm sorry, but I have an appointment in Arundel on Friday, and I'm not sure when I will be back. Don't worry. I shall find a way to make it up to you." He rose from his chair and kissed me lightly. He chuckled, no doubt at my look of disappointment.

# CHAPTER FOUR: SHADOWS OF THE PAST

Later that night I woke from a nightmare, my whole body shaking as I called out for my husband.

Sherlock shot up in bed and lit the taper candle. "What is it, Nene?" He stared at me anxiously.

"A bad dream," I said, smiling at him through tears.

He put his arm around my shoulder, holding me close. "It was more than that. There's clearly something on your mind. I am your husband. Pray tell me."

I sighed. "It's my cousin Beau. Even though I haven't seen him for years, he still tries to control my life. Last month I received a letter from my Uncle Aloysius. Apparently there was a dreadful scandal involving Beau and one of the ranch hands two years ago. Unfortunately the press got wind of it, and every sordid detail appeared in the Catskill Recorder. My uncle told Beau he had enough of his debauchery and ordered him to leave. Then Aunt Susannah left the ranch two months ago after telling my uncle what Beau did to me. My uncle apologised and asked for my forgiveness."

"And will you?" Sherlock raised an eyebrow.

"Yes." I nodded. "You have no idea how good it feels to be vindicated after all this time. So I think I can find it in my heart to forgive my uncle. And I would like to see my cousins Denis and Desmond again, although they probably have families by now."

"And your aunt and Beau?" he asked.

I shook my head. "I can never forgive my aunt for covering up what her son did. And as for Beau, as you know, he's a monster."

Sherlock rose from the bed. "Wait here," he said. "I shall be back in a moment."

Sherlock returned with a bottle of brandy and two glasses. He filled them before handing one to me. Then he took my hands in his and gazed at me intently. "Before we married, I vowed to keep you safe and find a way to bring your cousin to justice. And despite hiring an agent in New York, I have failed you. My agent told me Beau has likely committed similar crimes, but without witnesses prepared to come forward, it would be difficult to get a conviction. So I shall go myself to investigate further."

I shook my head. "I don't want you to do that," I said. "Beau is dangerous, and I couldn't bear it if anything happened to you. Promise me you won't go."

"If that's what you want," said Sherlock.

I sighed deeply. "My uncle's letter brought back memories. Demons from my past, which with your help and support, I had almost managed to forget. So I've decided to respond to my uncle's letter, but I'm not yet ready."

He kissed me on the cheek. "Come, let's go back to bed. You need to rest."

I lay in bed, comforted by my husband's soft breathing, his body warm beside me. Then I closed my eyes, and instantly I was back in the Catskills, the year 1873, as the memory of that fateful day came flooding back.

The summer of my fifteenth birthday saw a heatwave in the Catskills. The mercury climbed every day until it reached the nineties. The haying was underway, and the men toiled relentlessly in the fields, gathering early crops. I helped my Aunt Susannah in her vegetable garden, where we picked from an abundance of peas, summer squash, and cucumbers for my birthday supper later that evening.

My friend Betsy Drew from our neighbouring ranch baked me a cake, and Aunt Eileen sent me a beautiful silk dress of cornflower blue, with a sash and a bow to the side. I felt like a princess when I tried it on that afternoon. Betsy tied my hair in an elaborate chignon and applied a little make-up to my no doubt flushed cheeks.

After supper, my uncle and my cousins Denis and Desmond took Betsy home in the brougham, where they stayed for a while to have drinks with Betsy's father, Chuck. Beau didn't go with them. He'd been drinking heavily throughout the afternoon and my uncle had ordered him to bed.

Beau was my Aunt Susannah's son from her first marriage to Josh Walters, a cattle trader from Roxbury who died from typhoid when Beau was a baby. Susannah married my uncle two years later and he adopted Beau before he and Susannah went on to have two sons of their own — Denis and Desmond, such wonderful boys whom I loved dearly. Beau was different. Academically gifted, he lived in New York for most of the year and was a student at King's College. And, like me, he only came to the ranch during the holidays.

My mother died when I was a baby, and having seen off several governesses, who were all dreadful, my father didn't know what to do with me. So Aunt Eileen persuaded him to send me to my uncle's ranch in the Catskills, where I spent every summer, and I loved it. I became a spiritual orphan, running freely through the fields and mountains.

Denis and Desmond taught me to ride, shoot, and break in the quarter horses. Everything was perfect until Beau arrived that summer. Initially, I suppose, I was a little in awe of Beau — he was five years older, remarkably handsome, with a mane of thick black curly hair and large expressive brown eyes. We got on well at the start. We shared a love for Shakespeare and Percy Shelly. But one day he unexpectedly tried to kiss me. I was shocked, as I had no interest in him romantically. I only admired him.

I was fourteen, a child. I was also confused, as there was a rumour in the Catskills that Beau had a penchant for men. My cousin Denis confided in me that he'd once caught Beau in a compromising position with the farrier, Joe Jameson. After I spurned his advances, Beau turned against me, taking every opportunity he could to undermine me in front of my relatives. After that, I was wary of him and avoided being left alone in his company.

I was climbing into my bed when I heard a commotion coming from the direction of the stables. So I slipped on my dressing gown and slippers and headed to the stable block to investigate. My aunt's broodmare Pippi was expected to foal within the next few days, and I wanted to ensure all was well. I entered the stables to discover Pippi safely ensconced in her stable, munching away on grass hay.

I was disturbed by the sound of a creaking door. I turned around to discover Beau leering at me. "Well, Nene, you looked pretty as a picture today. All grown up in your new dress. I intend to steal a kiss from you," he drawled, laughing at my shocked expression. "Don't try to deny me, cousin, with your airs and graces. You're not too old to go over my knee for a whipping."

"Either would be as unpleasant as the other," I retorted.

Beau laughed again, although it was apparent that he was drunk. I believed he was teasing me at first, but then his smile vanished and his expression soured. He lurched toward me, grabbed hold of both wrists and pinned me against the wall. His lips came down on mine hard. I could smell the stench of his sweat, the stale aroma of whisky and cigarettes on his breath. I tried to push Beau away, but he was far too strong. He ripped the top of my nightdress, exposing my left breast.

"Stop! No!" I screamed. He released my wrists, then covered my mouth with one hand as he pulled a knife out of his pocket.

"Be still now," he hissed. "It'll be over soon. You might even enjoy it, Miss High-and-mighty." I found his laugh to be menacing as he unbuckled his belt and fumbled with the buttons on his trousers.

Having never before been touched by a man, let alone kissed, I was petrified. I instinctively kneed my cousin as hard as possible in the groin. He recoiled in agony before regaining his composure. Then he slapped me hard.

"Do that again and I'll slit your throat," he snarled.

I was shaking like a leaf and could feel bile rise in my throat as I realised what was about to happen. Then, out of the corner of my eye, I saw my aunt appear with a gun which she pointed straight at Beau's head.

"Let her go now, son." She pulled back the trigger, her voice calm.

Beau laughed. "And if I don't, what then?"

"Then I have no choice but to blow your head off like I warned you the last time this happened."

Beau reluctantly released his grip. He threw the knife onto the ground before walking out of the stable. Before he left, he turned to face me. "We have unfinished business, me and you, Nene. Don't ever forget that." He laughed bitterly.

"He'll be fine when he's slept it off. He can't handle the drink." My aunt covered my exposed body with her coat.

She took me back to the house and made me swear on the Bible not to speak of what happened to a living soul. She said no one would believe me if I did. I would only break my uncle's and father's hearts and sully my family's reputation.

After a family discussion a few days later, my Aunt Eileen intervened and persuaded my father to send me to a girl's boarding school in New York, and that was the last time I ever saw Beau, although the experience he put me through would stay with me for a lifetime. They say the ghosts of old adversaries die hard.

Sherlock arranged private counselling sessions after our marriage, and they helped for a while. My cousin Estelle argued that it must have been far worse being raped by my late husband Godfrey, and of course that was a horrendous experience. But I had forgiven Godfrey. Fuelled by his addictions and demons, he was as much of a victim as me. But Beau was far worse—he was an evil sexual predator. I have no doubt I would not have been his first or last victim, and that was something that always played on my mind. I felt guilty that I was unable to speak out about what happened. Sworn to secrecy by my aunt, and then sent to boarding school, I had nobody to confide in, no help or support to deal with the trauma.

The memories would appear unexpectedly and out of nowhere. A creaking door, the smell of whiskey, the aroma of certain colognes could trigger an episode. Those feelings of shame, terror, and hopelessness, as though Beau was in the room with me, continue to this day.

# CHAPTER FIVE: MEETING MARTHA HUDSON

Sherlock arrived late the following afternoon. He told me Mycroft had been delighted with his invitation.

I stared at him anxiously. "Promise me you *will* be civil to Mycroft. Could you try to be a little less you, even if only for one day?"

"Whatever do you mean?" Sherlock furrowed his brow. "I will be civil, although I cannot vouch for my brother's narrative. He never could resist trying to get one over me. But I'm sure he will be on his best behaviour in front of the children. And, if he isn't, then I will put him right."

"That's what worries me."

"It will be fine, you'll see. People say you can never escape your family." Sherlock chuckled. "On a lighter note, Mrs Hudson confirmed she's coming to help. I shall collect her from Amberley Station on Christmas Eve."

I breathed a sigh of relief. Sherlock wasn't too enamoured with my culinary skills, and I couldn't say I blamed him, having served him up several unmitigated disasters in the past. Soufflés and Yorkshire puddings that did not rise, burnt toast, and overcooked mutton. Not that he made a habit of complaining. My husband knew better than that. So I was relieved to learn that Martha was coming.

I first met Martha Hudson at the beginning of June. Due to the terrible experiences I'd endured years earlier with my first husband, Godfrey Norton, I always disliked London intensely.

I was, however, intrigued about Baker Street and tried to imagine what life must be like there, my husband being looked after by Mrs Hudson and the occasional visit from Doctor Watson. So I told Sherlock I wanted him to take me there. But, of course, he raised his concerns. We were aware of the risks if we were both discovered together by the underworld. So we chose a day when Mrs Hudson visited her sister in Brighton.

With me in the disguise of a gentlemen, we travelled separately by train to Victoria and then by tube to Baker Street. I wore a long black dress coat with a full collar, my hair tied up under a black beret. I disembarked at Stanmore before making my way to Baker Street, arriving ten minutes after my husband. I remembered, as if it was only yesterday, staring at the streetlamp outside the door of 221B, where I'd first seen Sherlock Holmes fiddling for his keys sixteen years earlier. Big Ben struck eleven as I entered the threshold and ran up the seventeen steps to find my husband anxiously waiting for me.

Walking into the large airy sitting room with two broad windows that looked down onto Baker Street was a breathtaking experience. I stood in the middle of the room and took everything in — the two comfortable-looking armchairs set by the fire, the chaise lounge on the opposite side, where Wilhelm Ornstein would have undoubtedly sat during his consultation in 1888.

My eyes scanned the wooden fireplace covered with letters and notes pierced by a jack-knife. My picture from La Scala held pride of place in the centre. To the left of the fireplace sat the strongbox where Sherlock kept my letters. Next sat a coal scuttle containing his cigars and a Persian slipper concealing his tobacco, all precisely as Sherlock had described.

I glanced around the room. My husband's Stradivarius violin was set in the corner, next to a table containing his magnifying glass, newspapers, chemicals, and equipment, besides a writing desk with various notebooks and the pen I had gifted to him in Fiesole.

Sherlock showed me the bedroom where Doctor Watson sometimes stayed. The room was neat and well organised, undoubtedly a relic of his days in the army. A door from the study led into my husband's bedroom, with its green walls and a medium-sized bed, a bedside table and a dressing table and wardrobe, heavy burgundy velvet curtains draped over the windows, and an Aubusson rug covering the wooden floor. This was a humbling moment and a fascinating insight into the mind of the world's greatest detective, who I was proud to call my husband, even if it couldn't be by name.

We had dinner that evening at Simpson's on The Strand before returning to Baker Street, where we sat around the fire sipping brandy, Sherlock's long legs stretched out in front of him.

"Are you glad you came?" He stared at me curiously as he struck a vestas match and lit his black clay pipe.

"Yes." I nodded. "When I return to Milan, I'll be able to imagine you here, Mrs Hudson fussing over you."

"I prefer it when *you* fuss over me." He sighed.

"Well," I whispered. "Perhaps we can make some memories together?"

We were awakened the following morning to the sound of the study door opening and a female voice singing as she went about her work.

"This can't be happening," cried Sherlock. "Mrs Hudson has arrived early."

"I wonder what your housekeeper will think about her illustrious tenant entertaining a lady in his bedroom?" I laughed at my husband's startled expression. "We *are* married with two children, for goodness sake. Mrs Hudson must know what happens in the marital bed."

"That's something I don't ever want to contemplate." Sherlock furrowed his brow.

We dressed quickly and entered the study, taking Mrs Hudson by surprise.

"Goodness, Mr Holmes, I wasn't expecting you."

"Evidently," he replied. "Mrs Hudson, allow me to introduce you to Nene, my wife."

"My husband insisted on showing me around," I said lamely, fighting a blush. There was no avoiding Mrs Hudson's ominous stare.

She smiled at me knowingly, taking in our dishevelled appearance with a glimmer of amusement. "I am delighted to meet you, Mrs Holmes. I polish your photograph every morning, so I feel as if I know you already." Martha chuckled. "I trust you slept well, my dear. Why, you are practically glowing! Shall I fetch you some breakfast?"

"We would love breakfast, thank you," I replied.

I had showered and tied up my hair when Martha returned with a tray containing a pot of steaming coffee, fresh rashers, eggs, and toast. Holmes and I devoured everything hungrily.

Martha beamed at me as she came to collect the breakfast dishes. "Your husband told me all about your children. I would love to meet them one day."

"Perhaps you could visit us at Christmas when the children are over from Milan?" Sherlock remarked over the remains of Mrs Hudson's stellar breakfast.

"Yes, I would like that very much," said Martha. "I'm more than happy to help. I shall be alone this year as my sister and her husband are away on a cruise."

"That would be splendid," said Sherlock. "The only stipulation is that you must call us Mr and Mrs Sapori, and we shall call you Martha. There can be no deviation. You do understand?"

"Yes." Martha broke into a wide grin. "I shall look forward to meeting the Sapori family."

# CHAPTER SIX: THE NIGHT BEFORE CHRISTMAS

Sherlock and I awoke early on Christmas Eve, disturbed by the sound of a brougham pulling up outside on the lane. I peered through the window, relieved to find it was Harold and his wife Molly, the proprietors of our local farm shop. They had come to deliver our festive order of meat and groceries, as well as holly and mistletoe. After breakfast, the children made crackers out of cardboard tubes they'd prepared earlier. They carefully stuffed the insides with sugared almond bonbons and covered them with brightly coloured paper before finally wrapping them together with mistletoe.

When the children had finished, I cut up what remained of the mistletoe. These plants had long been associated with surreptitious kisses symbolising fertility and romance. Well, we could all do with a little more romance in our lives. So I strategically placed the remaining sprigs over the doorway in Sherlock's study. Hopefully, with a little cajoling from me, my husband would enter into the spirit of the occasion. I knew I would have my work cut out, trying to bring out the romantic in him. But it was Christmas, and I was prepared to give it a go.

Next the children helped me make a holly wreath, an activity I'd always found to be a fun and rewarding experience for adults and children alike. Looking at the smiles of joy and happiness on the children's faces, I knew I was right. Nicco cut the red-and-green ribbon into eight-inch thin strips, carefully folding them in half. Charlotte pinched the ends, giving each a little twist, as Nicco fed them through the meshed fabric. The children followed me outside as I pinned the wreath onto our oak front door on the nail Sherlock had knocked in earlier. I explained to Nicco and Charlotte that the wreath was not merely a decoration, it was figurative and represented Christ's crown of thorns.

Later that morning, with all our Christmas tasks completed for now, Sherlock, the children, and I set out on an invigorating walk to the Three Tunnes Inn. The day was crisp and cold. Chalk cascaded from the cliffs like icing on a Christmas cake in the glorious winter sun. We stared ahead at the stunning vistas, disturbed by the sound of starlings screeching overhead.

When we arrived at the inn, Sherlock gave us a splendid luncheon of standing rib of beef with Yorkshire pudding, followed by cranberry and mince pie. To the children's delight, Joe, the pub landlord, played Christmas carols on the pianoforte while they sang along merrily.

When we returned to the farm, we took advantage of the low tide and took the footpath next to the river. The afternoon sun was reddening towards evening, a golden glimmer of sunlight cutting through the tall poplars and the blackening trees.

Charlotte, struggling to keep up with her father's long, purposeful strides, was delighted when he scooped her up and put her on top of his shoulders.

Nicco noticed a sack lying under a black poplar tree. Sherlock prodded it gently with his cane. When we heard a faint squeal., Nicco opened the bag to discover a chocolate brown Labrador puppy. The poor thing looked half-dead and shivered uncontrollably. Taking off my scarf, I wrapped it tightly around the stricken creature.

"Who on earth would do this?" I said, tears stinging my

eyes. "So much for the spirit of Christmas."

"It's a bitch," said Sherlock closely, inspecting the bedraggled puppy. "And most likely the runt of the litter, given its size. It would no doubt have drowned once the tide came in. I'm afraid it's the world's way in these parts."

"Well, when I find out who did this, they'll be getting a piece of my mind," I retorted.

"May I carry the puppy?" asked Nicco.

"Yes, of course. Put her under your coat to help keep her warm."

"Can we keep her, Mummy?" Charlotte peered over her father's shoulder, looking as though she was about to burst into tears.

"We'll see," I hesitantly replied, not wishing to give my daughter any false hope. It would be a miracle if the poor thing survived.

When we arrived back at the farmhouse, Sherlock immediately set off in the brougham to collect Martha from the station. Nicco found an empty crate he filled with straw, gently laying the puppy next to the kitchen fire, wrapped in a towel. The poor creature fell asleep immediately.

Nicco and Charlotte helped me prepare the mince pies. The aroma of dried fruit, spices, and brandy lingered in the air. I may not be the world's most incredible cook, but the baking skills I acquired in Violetta's kitchen in Fiesole nine years before stood me in good stead. I had already made a Christmas cake and a batch of buttermilk biscuits, although my husband had polished off most of them. When the minced pies were finally in the oven, I made a start on the Wassail punch, which was traditionally given to the carollers we were expecting that evening, members of the choir from our local church. I knew they were collecting for good causes, including a charity very close to my heart — Dr Barnardo's. So I added some extra cider into the mix, followed by a liberal dash of brandy. The children stirred in nutmeg, cinnamon, mixed spices, and slices of lemon, along with the olives I'd brought back from Milan. The punch smelt wonderful as it warmed through on the stove.

Sherlock finally returned from the station with Martha. I made a pot of fresh coffee which we consumed in the kitchen along with delicious hot minced pies fresh from the oven. Martha brought marbles for Nicco and a skipping rope for Charlotte. Sherlock persuaded Martha to try the punch. She took a sip. Furrowing her brow, she complained it too strong for her taste, explaining to the bemused children that she wasn't much of a drinker.

We were unexpectedly disturbed by Charlotte's sharp intake of breath. We turned around to discover the puppy we'd rescued had opened her eyes and was staring straight at Charlotte, wagging her tail, and our daughter was staring straight back with a look of the most profound affection in her beautiful blue eyes.

"Well," I said. "I believe this is what they call love at first sight."

"Knowing Charlotte, it's most likely trouble at first sight," Sherlock said.

We had barely finished our coffee when the carollers knocked at the door. Martha and I handed out cups of punch, while Nicco and Charlotte gave out the minced pies while singing along to Good King Wenceslas and Silent Night. Before the carollers left, Sherlock slipped some notes into their collection box.

With the children tucked up in bed, Martha and I decorated the dining-room table with linens, flowers, and evergreens to prepare for the dinner the following day. Martha refused Sherlock's sherry offer, explaining she was tired from the train journey and wished to retire early.

Later that evening, while listening to Wagner on the

gramophone and partaking in a glass of fine wine, I presented Sherlock with an oil painting of his musical idol, Paganini. My cousin Estelle, who looked after our main family home in Trenton, New Jersey, had bid for the artwork at Phillips auction house in New York and shipped it to me. The painting cost me far more than I anticipated. Still, it was a fine piece by George Paton, and it was worth every dollar to see the astonishment on my husband's face.

"It's a staggering piece of work," said Sherlock. "I notice something different each time I look at it." I followed him into the study and watched as he hung the picture on the wall facing his desk.

I thought it odd there was no mention of my gift, although I received a lingering kiss under the mistletoe for my trouble. I figured Sherlock had probably forgotten with all the excitement. Although I looked around our bedroom in all the prominent places, I found nothing. Not that I expected to.

# CHAPTER SEVEN: CHRISTMAS DAY

I woke earlier than usual on Christmas morning and reached for Sherlock to find his side of the bed empty. Then I remembered he'd risen early to attend to the horses.

I showered before stepping into the new dress I'd bought for the occasion and had shipped over from the House of Worth in France. The dress was silk, decorated with French lace, in soft colours of blue and beige. I went downstairs and lit the candles on the tree, concealing a glass pickle within its sturdy branches, before placing the children's Christmas presents underneath.

By the time Martha joined me, half an hour later, I was feeling a little flustered. Although delighted she was there to help, I realised I would have been entirely out of my depth with the cooking. Sherlock was right as ever.

"How does he always know?" I complained to Martha.

She laughed as she took control of the situation and began to expertly prepare the vegetables, potatoes, sage and onion dressing, and plum pudding. At the same time, I cooked us a splendid breakfast of bacon, eggs, and coffee with pancakes and fresh milk for the children. I even managed not to burn the toast.

Nicco and Charlotte had risen early with their father. They fed the chickens, collected their eggs, and attended to our two newly acquired kid nanny goats in the barn. They fussed over them for some time before Martha finally called them into the kitchen to wash their hands as I served up breakfast.

"The children are delightful. They're a credit to you."

Martha beamed over her coffee cup at their flushed little faces, bright with expectation and the excitement of the day.

After a leisurely breakfast, I took Nicco and Charlotte upstairs to bathe and change. Nicco was tall for his age and looked handsome in his black velvet court suit and white shirt, whilst Charlotte pulled a face through the pier-glass as I brushed her long black hair and plaited it, running scarlet ribbons through. I hoped to add a touch of elegance to our little tomboy before drawing a red lace dress with puffed sleeves and a fluttering sash over her head.

Charlotte looked beautiful, as bright as a butterfly, but I knew she would have preferred to be in dungarees and her favourite blue Wellington boots. Charlotte was never happier than when she was running around the farm and the fields with her father and Nicco, tending to the animals, jumping into puddles, and rolling around in the mud.

"It's only for one day, Charlotte, and please stop fidgeting." I laughed at her sombre expression. "We have an important guest coming for dinner, and I need you and your brother to be on your best behaviour."

"Who is Mycroft Holmes?" asked Nicco.

"He is a colleague of your father's. The brother of the celebrated consulting detective Mr Sherlock Holmes." Nicco brightened at my reply. He was a massive fan of Sherlock Holmes, having read all of Doctor Watson's chronicles in the Strand magazine. Nicco was so excited. He could hardly wait to meet our guest. Charlotte was less enamoured. I suspected she would have been far more interested if Mycroft had four legs and a tail.

Mycroft Holmes arrived by noon in an Oldsmobile roadster driven by his chauffeur who would collect him later that evening. Sherlock greeted Mycroft cordially, taking his hat and ulster before escorting him into the drawing room for a glass of rum punch.

I took the children into the drawing room to introduce them to Mycroft. Nicco, I could tell, was enthralled. Mycroft greeted us warmly, rising from his chair to kiss me on both cheeks. He was attired in a sombre black three-piece suit and wore a gold watch chain inside his waistcoat.

"Thank you for the invitation, Mrs Sapori. The gesture is much appreciated."

"Our pleasure," I replied, gesturing to my husband, who nodded dourly.

We watched as the children excitedly opened their presents — an atlas and a medical dictionary and chemistry set for Nicco, along with a Christmas book containing children's scientific experiments. Also a kaleidoscope and a rocking horse for Charlotte, as well as a stunning first edition *Alice's Adventures in Wonderland* by Lewis Carroll dated 1865, beautifully illustrated by Sir John Tenniel.

Mycroft brought a bottle of vintage port and Taittinger champagne for Sherlock and me. There was a clockwork train for Nicco and a lovely wax doll dressed in satins and lace for Charlotte. To the bemusement of my husband, the children presented Mycroft with a box of Cuban cigars, although Sherlock later told me in no uncertain terms that he thought it quite ridiculous that we should buy Mycroft a present.

We entered the dining room to find Martha serving the oyster starter, and Sherlock poured out the wine.

Mycroft beamed across the table at Nicco, appearing much taken with him. "Well, young man, pray to tell me, what would you like to do when you grow up?"

"I'm very interested in music and philosophy," said Nicco. "But I would like to be a surgeon."

"Splendid," said Mycroft before turning his attention to Charlotte. "And what of you, young lady? A nurse, I would fancy?"

"My sister would make an excellent nurse, Mr Holmes," interrupted Nicco. "But I think an even better doctor. Or perhaps a veterinarian."

"Is that right, Charlotte?" Mycroft smiled at her condescendingly.

"Yes." Charlotte nodded and smiled shyly. "I like animals very much, but I want to be a doctor so I can mend your sore knee and look after Mummy and Daddy when they're as old as you, Mr Holmes"

Mycroft stared at Charlotte, perplexed. Sherlock stifled a laugh. I glanced across the table at Nicco, who looked horrified. "My sister meant no offence, Mr Holmes. She merely refers to the arthritis that unfortunately afflicts you," explained Nicco. He stared at Mycroft anxiously.

"From the mouths of babes. How is your arthritis these days, Mycroft? Still playing you up, I see," said Sherlock sarcastically.

Mycroft responded with a grimace, flashing his brother a withering glance. He took a sip from his glass, wiping his lips with a napkin. "On the contrary," he said, smiling at the children. "It's comforting to know that my well-being will be in such capable hands in years to come. Although I'm not quite ready for my dotage."

Nicco appeared fascinated by Mycroft and could hardly take his eyes off him.

"Nicco," I whispered. "Come now, it's not proper to stare."

"I'm so sorry, mother." Nicco flamed crimson. "I wasn't aware I was doing it."

I slipped into the kitchen to help Martha carry the last dishes out onto the table for the main course. Mycroft insisted on carving the turkey and the beef, which Martha had cooked to perfection. She was apprehensive about joining us for dinner and had initially declined the invitation.

"I'll be fine in the kitchen," she said

I shook my head. "It wouldn't sit right with me if you didn't join us, considering all you do for my husband and this family."

Martha reluctantly conceded., although she later confided in me that she found Mycroft somewhat intimidating. I noticed he raised an eyebrow when she joined us at the table.

Holmes filled Martha's glass with wine.

"Merry Christmas," I said, raising my glass, everyone repeating the sentiment.

After dinner, the children insisted on playing parlour games, first Pass the Slipper, and then Blind Man's Bluff. Nicco won both games, much to Charlotte's exasperation. Next the children searched the Christmas tree, attempting to find the hidden glass pickle. Nicco stood on tiptoe, trying to reach the higher branches, but Charlotte's eagle eyes saw the pickle first. She laughed, mocking her brother, before running back into the parlour to retrieve her prize, which was a box of candies. When the children finally settled down, Mycroft asked me to play the pianoforte and I duly obliged. Everyone sat around the fireplace with a cup of hot chocolate, chestnuts roasting on the open fire, as I played first Wagner, then Beethoven, before Nicco joined me on the violin, singing along with Charlotte to "Once in Royal David's City". Charlotte finally persuaded a reluctant Mycroft to join in with the singing. Then I accompanied Nicco on the piano as he sang a beautiful solo, "The Minstrel Boy", an Irish patriotic song by Thomas Moore. I couldn't help but notice it brought a tear to Mycroft's eye.

We were all so engrossed by Nicco's stunning rendition that we failed to notice Charlotte slip out of the room until we heard a loud bang and a crash. Pandemonium quickly broke out in the Sapori residence. We dashed down the corridor towards the study. Holmes and Nicco reached the study first to find Charlotte wailing uncontrollably, tears rolling down her beautiful little face. The puppy Charlotte had named after Helen of Troy had crashed into the table holding Sherlock's scientific experiments and everything had fallen over. Glass and liquid littered the floor everywhere, and Helen, cowering in the corner, had peed on the floor.

Sherlock shook his head and sighed deeply. "Words fail me," he said, checking to see if Charlotte was injured. Thankfully she was fine, although her dress was saturated, the liquid trickling down onto her father's shirt. Nicco picked up Helen and discreetly returned her to the kitchen.

"I'm sorry, Daddy. Helen didn't mean it. She was only playing." Charlotte wailed.

"It's all right. It's my fault for not locking the door. But you need to take good care of the puppy. Otherwise Helen goes outside to the barn."

Charlotte nodded. Reassured by her father's words, she put her thumb in her mouth and laid her head on his shoulder.

"You look tired, young lady," said Sherlock. "Do you need an afternoon nap?"

"Yes," Charlotte murmured sleepily.

"I'll take her upstairs. I need to change my shirt," Sherlock remarked sharply, his face suffused with annoyance. "Today of all days! Mycroft must think we live in a madhouse."

Sherlock carried Charlotte upstairs to her bedroom and I followed, changing Charlotte out of her wet clothes before putting her down for her nap. Then I entered our bedroom to find my husband changing his shirt. He scowled at me through the pier glass.

"I cannot believe I let you talk me into having Mycroft over for Christmas. Before we know it, we'll be playing charades in the drawing room. Next year, we should invite the world and his wife and get another dog or cat. And why stop there? Let's have another baby. Two or three more children to add to the menagerie. Remind me again why I agreed to this madness?"

I recoiled at his words, shocked by his manner and the sarcastic tone in his voice.

Sherlock sighed deeply. "I'm sorry, Nene, I didn't mean that. You know I would never intentionally disrespect you."

"And yet you have." I glared at him. "That was low, even by your standards. I have neither the time nor the inclination to argue with you. We shall speak later."

I was furious. Sherlock and I had discussed having another child after Charlotte was born. That had caused many arguments between us. Charlotte's birth was traumatic — she was a breech baby. The umbilical cord became compressed during labour, leading to cord prolapse. It was only thanks to the skill and dedication of the midwife that we didn't lose our beautiful little girl.

Sherlock was naturally concerned that something might happen to the child, or me, should I become pregnant again. He argued that it would not be fair on Mycroft, who footed the bill for the children's security. How could I argue with that because, as always, my husband was right? So, in the end, I reluctantly conceded. Of course I knew that his irritability and restlessness were all compounded by the lack of an intriguing case to occupy his great brain. Intelligence and troubled minds often go hand in hand. I knew from personal experience that my husband could become annoying and insufferable at such times. But, even so, it had been a while since I'd seen him so vexed or felt so uncomfortable in his presence.

Naturally he was pleased that the children and I could live our lives without discord or enmity. Yet whenever Sherlock came close to that level of alleviation, without a mystery to investigate, his tortured intensity would manifest itself and his mood would darken, craving adventure and excitement as if it was a drug. To Sherlock, life without a challenge was like a meal with no seasoning on a day without sunshine.

At times my husband's tendency to say what he was thinking was disquieting. Especially if you weren't always ready to hear what he had to say. Although, on a more positive note, he never lied. Over the years, Sherlock's general demeanour had greatly improved. I knew he would never dream of speaking to me in such a way under normal circumstances. I wouldn't be with him if he did.

Before we embarked upon a relationship, our burgeoning friendship, fuelled by our shared love of music, was fiery and intense, and we had several heated altercations. Still, I always gave as good as I got, which I believe was one of the reasons Sherlock was attracted to me in the first place. He was a man unused to being challenged by anyone, let alone the fairer sex, finding most women inscrutable.

My friend Sophia asked me once what I saw in Sherlock. And I explained that he was quite unlike any man I'd ever met before, unafraid of anything or anyone, a man devoid of self-doubt, confident in his sagacity. While his behaviour could be eccentric and challenging at times, I never once doubted his love and devotion to the children and me. At least not until now.

Having no wish to create a scene in front of the children and our guests, I entered the bathroom to splash cold water on my face and fix my make-up, composing myself before going downstairs to find Martha mopping the study floor.

"You shouldn't be doing this," I said. "You deserve a break as much as anyone else."

"Nonsense," said Martha. "I will have it done in an instant. I have had years of experience cleaning up after your husband." She laughed.

31

# CHAPTER EIGHT: MYCROFT AND ME

Entering the drawing room, I was surprised to find Mycroft sitting alone.

"I'm sorry," I said. "I thought my husband and Nicco would be here to entertain you."

"Your husband and Nicco have gone to the stables. Is it always this chaotic? Your daughter appears to be a rather wilful child."

"It is, at least where Charlotte is concerned." I furrowed my brow, suddenly feeling the need to defend my daughter from Mycroft's patronising comments. "She can be a handful at times, but I wouldn't have her any other way."

"Forgive me. I am unused to children and family life. But I do find the children utterly charming and precocious, both as smart as whips."

"Yes," I agreed. "And I think we both know who they take after."

Mycroft chuckled. "Indeed," he said. "While we are on our own, Nene — may I call you Nene?"

"Well, it is my name."

"I wish to apologise once more for my behaviour in Fiesole. I was, of course, trying to protect my brother, as I have done all my life. But what I didn't understand then was how strong the bond was between you."

"I did try to explain."

"Yes, I know. I'm sorry. Even the cleverest of people make mistakes sometimes."

"Let's put it behind us." I offered him a smile. "No one can change the past. All we can do is embrace the future."

"Absolutely." Mycroft raised his glass. "I'll drink to that."

Nicco entered the room. "Mother, I'm sorry to interrupt, but father has asked if you can help him at the stables. He said one of the horses has gone wrong."

"Ah, yet another crisis." Mycroft arched an eyebrow in mock humour. "Well, there's certainly never a dull moment around here, my dear. With your domestic woes, the staff joining us for dinner, and then your husband having to oversee the horses, who I must say demand an extraordinary amount of attention. If I didn't know better, I would suggest Mr Sapori was trying to avoid me."

"Not at all. I'm afraid I am at fault for allowing the servants time off, and today of all days." I gave him a half-hearted laugh.

"As loyal as ever, I see. Your husband chose well when he took you for his wife. Please go to him, don't worry about me. I'm sure this young man is more than capable of keeping me entertained." Mycroft smiled at Nicco.

"Would you like to play chess, Mr Holmes?" Nicco asked.

"Why not." Mycroft chuckled as Nicco ran off to get the chess set.

I smiled at him sardonically. "My son may only be eight years old, but underestimate him at your peril. In the matter of chess, Nicco will be no match for you, but at least he will give you a run for your money."

"I will bear that in mind, Nene, thank you." Mycroft stared at me with a whimsical expression.

I left Nicco and Mycroft to set up the chessboard and made my way towards the stables, wondering what could have happened. I took a breath before crossing over the threshold. How I had been dreading this day. Over the years, my relationship with Sherlock had been exceptional. He worked hard to present the best version of himself before the children and me, but perhaps now was the time to release him from his obligations. So, with a heavy heart, I slipped into the stable block where I found Sherlock loading hay in one of the mangers.

"Which of the horses has gone wrong?" I quizzed, staring at him anxiously.

A shadow of a smile passed over Sherlock's face. "Ah, sorry to have alarmed you, but I needed to draw your attention somehow. I've been trying to get you out here all day. Come with me." He took my hand and led me towards the end stall, which usually stood empty.

Sherlock slowly pushed open the door. I was stunned to find a black Friesian yearling, a small white star on his forehead, lying in the straw, gazing back. I was speechless as my husband and I entered the stall, sitting down beside the yearling who pricked up his ears as I stroked his head and thick black mane.

"For me?" I murmured. "I thought you'd forgotten my Christmas present. My god, he is magnificent."

"I do pay attention some of the time." Sherlock chuckled, staring at me keenly. "You have no idea how long I deliberated over him. I almost chose a filly who was a bonny thing, but then decided this little chap had more spirit. His official title is Black Hawk Gallo, but what will you name him?"

"Well." I laughed. "As I failed to notice your plan, I shall call him Shadow. How did you get him here?"

"He was delivered yesterday while we were at the Three Tunnes. The children were in on the secret. They've been helping me to look after him."

I sighed. "You can be exasperating at times, Mr Holmes. But, even after all these years together, there are moments like this when you do something that reminds me again why I love you. I would never want to be with anyone else."

"Yes," said Sherlock, as he stared into my eyes. "I have no idea what I did to deserve you either, Nene. Do you think I'm not aware of the sacrifices you've made so we can be together? The way you put up with my moods and insensitivities, like the incident earlier. I had no right to say that to you. Forgive me?"

When I nodded, he sighed. "Mycroft always brings out the worst in me. How you can excuse my brother's behaviour after he forced us apart for over four years amazes me. People consider love the most challenging emotion, but they're wrong. It's regret, that gnawing feeling eating away at you, reminding you of what you had and lost. Those years we were apart I consider the biggest failure of my life. So if you can find it in your heart to forgive Mycroft, I must find a way to come to terms with your decision."

I nodded. "Your brother was only trying to protect you, and I understand that now. Let's put it behind us and celebrate what we have. But, you know, I'm glad Mycroft got to see the children. The security he provides to keep them safe is immeasurable." I paused for a moment, gazing into my husband's eyes. "I would never want you to stay with me out of a sense of duty. If the drama of family life becomes too much for you, then you need to tell me. I will accept whatever you say, for I know you would never lie to me."

Sherlock smiled, tears running down his cheeks. "You are a remarkable woman, Nene. Every day I remind myself of that fact, and how fortunate I am to be your husband and a father to those two incredible children. Love came to me late and unexpectedly. First you, then Nicco and Charlotte. Unexpected, yes, but never unwanted. And to be allowed to return that love is the most incredible privilege. I know I rarely tell you this, but I love and adore you with my whole heart. I want you to know that."

I put my arms around him and hugged him, tears in my own eyes. And as I did so, I realised how blessed I was to lead such an incredible, sometimes lonely, but often exhilarating life. For Sherlock and me, being together wasn't always easy. We made a lot of sacrifices along the way to maintain our relationship. A lot of strategic planning was involved, often with the help and support of Mycroft, and all for one purpose — to keep our children safe. But, as far as Sherlock and I were concerned, Nicco and Charlotte always came first.

Our time together in Fiesole, and our confrontation with Colonel Moriarty, made me acutely aware of how fragile life was, and the importance of friends and family, even disordered family members. Admittedly, Mycroft might be pompous and cantankerous at times, but like his brother, under that icy exterior was a decent man who I knew would be prepared to do anything for our children, despite the fact he only met them for the first time that day. So I decided I could cope with his sardonic humour and his sanctimonious comments. After all, it wasn't as though I would be expected to entertain him every day.

# CHAPTER NINE: THE SPIRIT OF CHRIST-MAS PAST

The children were tucked in bed by seven, exhausted from the day's excitement.

I was on my way downstairs when I heard a rapping at the front door. I opened it to discover a tall, slim, elegant-looking lady with long jet-black hair swept into an elaborate up-do. Her sparkling blue eyes stared at me under a wide-brimmed black silk hat. The long black velvet coat could not conceal that she was heavily pregnant.

"I'm sorry to disturb you at this late hour," she said. "But I'm looking For Lucca Sapori. I must speak to him on a matter of the utmost importance."

"And who, may I say, is asking for him?"

"My name is Libertas James. Tell him it's Libby. He will know who I am."

"Please come in." I escorted Libertas into the lounge, politely asking her to take a seat. "I shall tell Mr Sapori you're here," I said before leaving the room, my heart beating wildly.

In all the time I'd known my husband, he'd never once given me cause to doubt him. Over the years, I'd caught other women eyeing him, especially at La Scala when he looked so striking in his formal evening wear. However he always appeared oblivious to their attentions. But, even so, I couldn't help wondering who this mysterious woman was and what she could want with my husband. All sorts of wild imaginings flooded my brain as I entered the drawing room, where

I found Mycroft and Sherlock sitting listening to Wagner on the gramophone, enjoying a cigar and a glass of port.

I cleared my throat before speaking, my voice shaky. "A lady, heavy with child, is in the lounge asking for Lucca Sapori." I stared at my husband desperately, trying to gauge his reaction.

"A pregnant woman asking for me, you say?" Sherlock furrowed his bow and stared at me incredulously. His eyes sharpened through the blue mist of tobacco smoke. "Did this woman give a name?"

"Libertas James. You may know her as Libby."

My husband and Mycroft looked at each other in astonishment. Mycroft shook his head. "Indeed, there is some mistake, surely. That cannot be."

"We will soon find out." Sherlock stubbed out his cigar and walked purposely towards the lounge, swiftly followed by Mycroft and me.

I entered the lounge with some trepidation to find my husband and Libertas James embracing warmly, her arms wrapped around his neck as she kissed him tenderly. They say jealousy is as fierce as the grave. It felt as though my whole world had imploded as I watched Libertas James walk over to Mycroft and embrace him, also.

My husband chuckled, observing my perplexed expression. "It's all right, Nene. I can assure you, this is not what it appears. I struggle to choose between two types of shag tobacco, never mind another woman. Please allow me to introduce you to my sister."

Libertas stepped forward and kissed me on both cheeks. "I apologise for the dramatics," she said breathlessly. "But I didn't know who was in your house, and I didn't want to ask for my brother by name, in case I exposed who he was. I've been following him for weeks until I was finally able to discover his secret identity."

"Why don't you come through to the drawing room? There's a fire, and Martha can get you a hot drink to warm you."

Libertas nodded, and a faint smile appeared on her face. "You're very kind. Please call me Libby. I don't even have to ask who you are, your photographs do you no justice. I hope my brother knows how fortunate he is to have you for his wife."

"I'm forever reminding my husband of that, but then I do consider myself the fortunate one." I smiled at Sherlock. "Would you like me to leave you with your siblings? You must have a lot of catching up to do."

"No need." Sherlock shook his head. "I think we should all hear what my sister has to say."

We retired to the drawing room. Martha brought in hot chocolate for Libby, and I took a small glass of dry sherry while Mycroft and Sherlock topped up their glasses with port. Martha discreetly retreated into the kitchen.

Libby took a sip from her cup and let out a long sigh before speaking, focusing her attention on me for much of the conversation, no doubt attempting to avoid Mycroft's piercing stare. "From the expression on your face when I first came in, Nene, I assume you know nothing of me?"

"No." I shook my head. "I'm sorry, but I don't."

"That's understandable." Libby nodded. "Allow me to introduce myself. I am the black sheep of the Holmes family, forever a cause of embarrassment to my brothers." She laughed derisively. "My mother died giving birth to me, and I don't think Mycroft ever forgave me for that, did you, dear brother?"

"Don't be ridiculous." Mycroft stared at his sister aghast.

"I'm sorry I let you down and was such a perpetual disappointment," said Libby before returning her gaze to me. "Apparently my mother was a paragon of virtue, everything I am not. How could I ever hope to live up to that? I decided not to waste one second trying." She scoffed. "Our father succumbed to cancer when I was eight years old, and I was officially an orphan. I became Mycroft's ward."

Libby paused for a moment, taking a sip from her cup before continuing. "My brothers did what they thought was best for me. I attended a private girls boarding school before winning a place to study mathematics and classics at London University."

"Yes," said Mycroft. "You graduated with a double first and had a glittering career before you. Then you wasted it by running away with your tutor, Alun James."

Libby glared at her brother, her eyes flashing like embers. "We loved each other. We asked your permission to marry. You told us it was out of the question because Alun was older and had been married before. You decided we couldn't be together. But Alun was a widower and a good man."

"You absconded to New York without a word," said Mycroft. "Have you any idea how concerned we were? We made extensive enquiries before we finally discovered you and James had married."

"So you decided to wash your hands of me," said Libby.

I could see she was close to tears.

"What could we do?" Mycroft threw up his hands. "All our letters were returned unopened. As far as we were concerned, you made your bed and you should lie in it. So we decided the only thing we could do was leave you to get on with it. And by the looks of it, you've done precisely that." Mycroft gestured with disdain to his sister's expanding stomach.

Sherlock was sitting with his legs crossed. He'd barely said a word but listened, as was his custom, with closed eyes and fingertips together. He glanced over towards his sister, a wary expression on his face. "Why are you here, Lib? It's certainly not to wish us the season's compliments."

Libby sighed. "You know me too well, brother. I've come to ask for your help, you and your wife."

"What do you mean?" I, stared at Libby curiously.

She put her hand on her stomach. "I only returned to England to put this child up for adoption."

"Why on earth would you do that?" I stared at her aghast. "You're married, for goodness sake."

Libby grimaced. "Before I married my husband, he made it perfectly clear he didn't want more children. He already had two girls from his first marriage. But I loved Alun so much that I agreed to his terms. We were happy together. I was an excellent stepmother to his two daughters, Sabrina and Emily. But then, earlier this year, I discovered I was pregnant. I knew then what I had to do, what would be expected of me."

"But surely, once your husband discovered you were with child, he had second thoughts? Children are a gift, not merely a consequence of the marriage bed," I expounded, barely able to believe what I was hearing.

Libby shook her head. "No, Alun was adamant that he did *not* want the child. I even considered getting an abortion, but then I changed my mind at the last minute. I might be many things, but I am no infant murderess."

"Thank goodness for that, at least," I said, horrified. "But how can we be of help to you?"

"I discovered that you have two children. and from what I've seen, you appear to be excellent parents. I want you to adopt my son."

"How on earth can you possibly know it's a boy?" cried Sherlock.

"I just do."

Sherlock shook his head. "I'm nearly fifty years old, Lib. You have no idea how difficult it is at times for my wife and me to live this life of duplicity. Our children will be at boarding school in a few years, and I hope to retire before I'm sixty. That will be our time, mine and Nene's. Our time to discover new adventures together. I owe her that, at least. So the answer to your question, I'm afraid, is a resounding no."

"What about you?" I stared at Mycroft. "Surely you could take the child and hire a nanny, or a governess, at least until the child is old enough to attend school?"

"No," Libby interrupted, shaking her head. "Mycroft did his best for me when I was a girl, and I'm grateful to him, but I don't want this child to live through the strict regime I was subjected to. That's one of the reasons I left. If none of you will help me, I will have little choice but to put the child up for private adoption."

Sherlock stared hard at Libby. "If you want our help, don't be mendacious. This child is certainly not your husband's."

Libby appeared taken aback for a moment. Her face turned pale and she shook her head, blinking hard. "No, you're right. You could always tell when I was lying. I must be mad thinking I could get anything past you and Mycroft. But don't you see, this is how desperate I have become."

"Tell us exactly what happened. And don't lie to us again." Mycroft leaned forward in his chair, his lip curled in disdain.

Libby took another sip from her cup before continuing. "In October of last year, Alun and I separated. We'd been arguing a great deal. I had turned thirty-eight and decided I wanted a child of my own. When I told Alun, he took the news badly. He was nearly sixty and said he was too old to start again. I did everything to persuade him, but he was adamant. So, in the end, I felt compelled to leave him. I moved away from our home in Cobble Hill and rented an apartment in Manhattan. Then I accepted a position as a mathematics teacher at Trinity school. That's where I first met Rick Munroe, a fellow schoolmaster of English literature. We soon embarked on a torrid affair. Rick was enigmatic, clever, and ridiculously handsome. His face had perfect symmetry." Libby sighed. "I was delighted to discover we had much in common — romantic poets, literature, and art. He was even left-handed like me." She laughed. "Everything was perfect between us, or so I thought. Then one day, I arrived home early and found Rick in bed with a boy, one of his pupils, and I couldn't cope with that. Another woman perhaps, but a boy, how could I possibly compete?"

Mycroft stared at his sister in stunned disbelief. "You caught your lover in bed with an innocent child, and your first thought was how it could affect you? Unbelievable."

"I know, it sounds terrible when you put it like that. Admittedly, it wasn't my finest hour. Rick and I were never going to walk off into the sunset together. But even so, I expected more from him. I was appalled by his behaviour, and I threatened to report him to the headmaster. Rick told me not to bother. He'd already decided to leave the school. He stormed out of the apartment, but he came back to see me one last time." Libby bit her lip hard. "You see, Rick had taken compromising pictures of me while we were together that he had developed himself. He said he would not hesitate to send them to Alun and the school if I ever revealed what I'd seen."

Mycroft stared at his sister in horror, a look of the utmost contempt on his face. "How could you be so stupid? Have you no shame?"

Libby shook her head. "I had no sense of shame where that man was concerned. Our affair was passionate and intense. I know it was wrong, and I am sorry, Mycroft. But I was devastated that someone I was once so close to could treat me as such, although I suspected he'd done it before. There was something in his cocksure manner, the way he spoke to me. Rick said he would teach me a lesson I would never forget, and if I crossed him again, he would come back and kill me. I thought Rick was bluffing at first to scare me, but the next day, I found my cat, Matilda, dead — her throat cut, her blood and entrails smeared all over my kitchen."

"This is outrageous," cried Mycroft. "You should have contacted us. Or at the very least reported him to the police."

Libby nodded. "I know that now, but I wasn't thinking clearly then. And when I thought things couldn't possibly worsen, I discovered I was with child." She took a deep breath before she continued, sipping from her cup. "A few weeks later, I received a letter from Alun. He told me he wanted to see me to discuss our future. He told me he wanted me back — he would do anything, even give me a child if necessary. I laughed in Alun's face and told him it was far too late. I had little choice but to tell him about Rick and my pregnancy, although I didn't mention the photographs. Alun was mortified. Once he recovered from the initial shock, he said he would take me back, but I must have the baby adopted. I was devastated, of course, as I knew this was my only chance to have a natural child. What could I do? I had no intention of raising the baby on my own. I was too selfish for that. And I didn't want to lose my husband."

"I cannot believe what you're saying," I said, appalled by her every word.

"Come, Nene," said Libby, speaking in a sneering tone. "It's obvious you love my brother. The chemistry and affection between the two of you is obvious. Are you telling me you wouldn't make sacrifices for him?"

"I've made plenty of those, I can assure you." I scoffed. "You have no idea what Sherlock and I have endured together. But I would never give up my children for anyone, not even him. They are my greatest blessing. Where is your husband now?"

"He's back home in the States. I've been here for four months. We didn't want our friends or any of Alun's family to find out about the pregnancy. When the child's born, I'll return to my husband and the girls. No one will be any the wiser."

I shook my head. "I don't understand how your husband could let you come all this way on your own while carrying a child. What kind of man is he?"

"I think we're about to find out," said Sherlock blandly as he rose from his seat, parted the blinds, and looked out through the window. "We're about to be visited by an esteemed American. An automobile has pulled up outside. The driver is wearing a New York chauffeur's badge. I think we can safely assume that the occupant of this vehicle is your husband." He glanced towards his sister, who wore a bewildered expression.

There was a sharp pull at the bell, followed by a loud definitive knock. Sherlock walked into the hallway. We heard harsh words exchanged for several minutes before my husband returned to the room, a grim expression on his face, followed by our eminent guest. Alun was a tall, grey-haired, distinguished-looking man with a beard, attired in an Inverness cloak and an immaculately brushed black felt hat, which he doffed and then bowed with an air of dashing melancholy.

"Thank God." He smiled at Libby with a look of profound tenderness before holding her in a loving embrace. "I've been trying to reach you for weeks. Why did you not return any of my letters?"

"I wanted it to be over," sobbed Libby. "Why are you here, Alun?"

"I had to see you. I couldn't bear being without you. The girls miss you dreadfully."

"Where are they now?"

"They're with my sister. When I arrived at the hotel this afternoon, the concierge told me you'd already left. My chauffeur followed you here and revealed your whereabouts."

"Forgive me," I said, excusing myself. "I need to go and

check on the children."

I ran upstairs to the children's room. Nicco and Charlotte were sleeping soundly, I kissed them both on the cheek. I couldn't bear to think of a day when I wouldn't have them in my life. Sherlock had been right all along. It was selfish of me even to consider having another child. It would be madness to risk our children growing up without a mother. I, of all people, knew how that felt.

I was about to go downstairs when I saw Sherlock come out of our bedroom.

"Are you all right, Nene?"

I shook my head. "No, not really. I don't understand what's going on with your sister and why you and your brother didn't offer her more support."

Sherlock sighed deeply. "We were trying to make her face her responsibilities. My sister is selfish, she always has been. Do you think Mycroft and I would stand by and allow our nephew to be adopted? That is never going to happen. After you left the room, Lib told me that she had no wish to see the child. She said it would be too difficult."

"I bet she did," I said. "But, don't you see, Libby is only saying this to please her husband. There's no way she wants to give up her child. We have to find a way to make her realise that before it's too late."

Sherlock nodded. "Come, let's go downstairs and find out what is happening."

We entered the drawing room to find Mycroft and Alun staring at each other in stony silence.

I noticed a pool of water on the floor by Libby's feet. "Are you all right?" I asked, speaking to her softly. "It looks as though your water has broken. Do you think you can make it upstairs? We need to get you somewhere more comfortable."

Libby looked down and began to sob. Martha and I escorted Libby to the guest bedroom, where I handed her a clean nightgown.

I turned to Martha. "We could do with a midwife, but we don't have time for that. Have you delivered a child before? As I don't think the men will be of much use."

"As a matter of fact, I have." Martha smiled triumphantly. "My youngest sister, Edith. It was long ago, but the principle remains the same. We are going to need hot water and clean towels."

I slipped into the bathroom, quickly returning with both, although another few hours passed as Libby's contractions became more frequent. Martha checked the clock on the wall. They were coming every two minutes now. Libby squeezed my hand tightly as another contraction deftly arrived and she cried out in agony.

"Push, my dear," said Martha, as Libby gave a guttural groan and the head appeared with a shock of black hair.

"Please push again," cried Martha.

Libby grimaced. She pushed once more as Martha cradled the baby, guiding him out of the womb and onto a towel. Martha smacked the baby's bottom, forcing him to take a breath. She wrapped him up carefully, cutting the cord with a pair of nail scissors, and he let out a piercing yell.

I gazed at him. He was so beautiful. He reminded me of Nicco when he was born.

Libby turned her face to the wall. "I don't want to see him. Please take him away."

At that moment, Alun burst into the room. He took hold of Libby's hand and kissed her on the cheek. "I'm so sorry for all you're endured. But everything will be back to normal soon, you'll see."

I glared at him. "You think you've lost everything because of this child? You have no idea." Gently taking the baby from Martha, I walked to Libby's bedside. "Here is your son," I said. "I want you to look at him. If you can do that and then

47

tell me you don't want him, then fair enough, your brother and I will raise him as our own." I placed the baby in Libby's arms. Then Martha and I swiftly left the room, locking the door behind us. We stood still like two statuettes, eavesdropping on their private conversation.

Deadly quiet reigned for several minutes. Then Alun spoke first. "My God, Libby, look at him. He's beautiful. He looks like you. The resemblance is staggering."

"Yes, he does," Libby agreed. Her voice faltered as she began to cry.

"How could we even consider giving him up?" said Alun. "I don't know what I was thinking turning my back on the boy. He's just an innocent child. I'm prepared to accept and raise him as my son if you'll allow it, Lib."

Libby gasped. "Are we to take him home?"

"Yes," said Alun. "Together we shall tell the girls that they have a new brother."

I discreetly unlocked the bedroom door before Martha and I made our way downstairs.

Then I asked the James's chauffer John Barnaby to drive me to the thatched cottage half a mile away, the home of our neighbours Alfred and Jayne Crawshaw. My friend Jayne had given birth to beautiful twin boys three months earlier. After I explained the situation, Jayne kindly gave me a bag of baby clothes, diapers, and a wicker bassinet with blankets. I was so grateful. The weather forecast predicted snow the following morning, and I knew it would be difficult to get into town to buy provisions.

Mycroft's chauffeur had arrived by the time I returned to Ash Tree Farm. However, due to the lateness of the hour and the inclement weather forecast, Mycroft agreed to Sherlock's request to drop Martha off at Baker Street. I thought it was the least he could do after she'd safely delivered his nephew into the world. Although I suspected Mycroft was keen to return to the peace and tranquillity of the Diogenes Club.

Mycroft turned to me before getting into the car and kissed me on both cheeks. "Thank you again for your hospitality, Nene. This has certainly been a Christmas I'll not forget in a hurry. I've made my peace with my sister, and I now have another fine nephew." He chuckled.

"I'm glad you came," I said. "I want to thank you for everything you do for the children."

"I consider it an honour and a privilege." Mycroft raised his hat. "Now, if you will excuse me, I'll bid you and your charming family a good evening and the season's compliments."

Sherlock and I waved goodbye to Mycroft and Martha as the car pulled away. My husband retired to the drawing room with Alun while I ran upstairs to check on Libby. I found her fast asleep, holding the baby in her arms. After gently removing the child and laying him in the bassinet, I slipped one of the baby dresses over his head before wrapping him up in a blanket.

Martha had made him a diaper from a towel she'd cut into pieces, fastening it expertly with a safety pin. I was about to slip out of the room when Libby jolted awake from her nap. She asked if I would sit with her for a moment. I nodded, taking a seat in the chair beside the bed.

"Are you all right?" I asked

"Yes, I'm fine. Thank you for all you've done for my son and me."

"You are more than welcome. But I think you and Alun should stay here for another day. Snow's coming tomorrow and I don't think it will be safe to travel with a baby. Your husband's chauffeur is welcome to stay here as well."

"Thank you, Nene. You're too kind."

I stared at Libby curiously. "Tell me, what was Sherlock like when he was younger? I often wonder what it would have been like to have known him then."

Libby smiled at me. "Well, if you can believe it, my brother was far more uptight and intense than he is now. Although I can tell he's different when he's with you. He's kinder, and better with people. He was a handsome young man." She laughed. "No doubt about it, he was full of himself, adopting an air of boorish arrogance from an early age. But I remember when I was at boarding school, Sherlock would come to see me every Sunday. We would take long walks together before he gave me luncheon. He was never as overbearing or as strict as Mycroft. I looked up to him. He was the closest thing I had to a father. Don't get me wrong, I love Mycroft. But without a wife to guide him, he was entirely out of his depth trying to raise a child. Despite Sherlock's peculiarities and eccentricities, I adored him. He was never dull. I would have done anything for my brother back then, as I would now. Although, I often drove him to distraction if, God forbid, I ever dared to interrupt the thread of his thoughts. Or worse still, one of his scientific experiments. Then there would be hell to pay. But his bark was always worse than his bite. He never once raised his hand to me."

"Same with our children, although admittedly he would never need to. One glare from those magnetic eyes would be enough to keep Nicco and Charlotte in check." We laughed. "May I offer you some light refreshment?"

"Tea would be excellent. And perhaps a sandwich. If that's not too much of an imposition." Libby glanced over towards the bassinet. "I guess my son will be fine for a while. I put him to my breast before you came in, and he took to it well."

"Good, I'm glad. Have you thought of a name?"

"Yes. We've decided to call him Ruben Alun." Libby stared at me curiously. "May I ask you a question, Nene?"

"Of course."

"Are you related to the Adlers from Livingston Manor

from the Catskills by chance?"

"Yes, Aloysius is my uncle. Why do you ask?"

"A friend of mine embarked on a personal relationship with his son Beau. One that ended in tears, I'm afraid. She said he liked to pop a cork, and when he did, he turned into a monster."

"Your friend is all right, I hope?" My voice was low, speaking almost in a whisper.

"Yes, thankfully she managed to get away from him."

"Thank goodness," I said, staring at her grimly. "It gives me no pleasure to tell you that Beau is my stepcousin. I, too, had an episode with him when I was younger. Thankfully, my aunt intervened before it got out of hand."

"I'm sorry to dredge up the past. I didn't realise you were so closely related."

"Don't worry." I smiled. "I've managed to put it behind me. I'm sure your friend will too. However, I'd hate to think that Beau is still subjecting other women—and perhaps men—to what I had to endure. Sherlock said it would be difficult to prove anything unless other women came forward. But, of course, that's never going to happen."

"You never know. Miracles do happen."

I excused myself and slipped downstairs to the kitchen, having no wish to continue our conversation about Beau. That brought back old memories I wanted to forget. I returned with a tray of Earl Grey, a ham sandwich, and a mince pie. I shut the bedroom door gently behind me and was surprised to discover the children standing on the landing.

"I'm sorry," said Nicco. "But Charlotte and I were disturbed by the sound of voices. We heard a baby cry."

"Do we have a new brother or sister?" Charlotte, wide-eyed, looked at me expectantly.

"No, nothing like that." I laughed. "But we have a guest who has just given birth to a baby boy. Would you like to see him?" The children nodded.

"Come along then." I put my finger to my lips. "But please be quiet. We must not wake him." We slipped into the bedroom to find Libby sipping tea. "I'm sorry to disturb you. The children are awake. They would like to see the baby, if you raise no objections."

"No, of course not," said Libby.

Charlotte peered into the crib. "I wish he was ours." She sighed. "Is he the baby Jesus?" She starred in wonder at Libby.

"Don't be ridiculous, Charlotte." Nicco looked at his sister with disdain. "You know perfectly well when Jesus was born."

"Yes," Charlotte replied indignantly. "But he promised to come back."

"No, I can categorically say that my son is not Jesus." Libby laughed. "But this little boy is your cousin, and I am your aunt Libby, your father Lucca's sister. I'm delighted to make your acquaintance. Well, don't just stand there." She chuckled at the children's puzzled expressions. "Come hug your aunt."

Charlotte walked tentatively to the bed, followed by Nicco. Libby embraced them both, tears of joy in her eyes. The children happily chatted to Libby for ten minutes before I insisted they return to bed. Otherwise, I knew they would not get up in the morning. I tucked them back in bed before slipping downstairs, finally joining my husband in the drawing room.

"There you are. After the day you've had, I fancy you could use a drink," said Sherlock.

I nodded. "Yes, thank you. A glass of wine would not go amiss." I sank into my chair, kicking off my shoes as I relayed to Sherlock all that had transpired.

He stared at me curiously as I sipped from my glass. "Tell me, were you really going to do it? Take on my sister's child?"

"Yes."

"Why?"

"Because as disordered as the Holmes family is, that little boy is part of us. He is your nephew, our children's cousin, and I couldn't stand by and not do anything. I knew Libby would have second thoughts when she saw him. She never wanted to give him up in the first place."

Sherlock nodded. "Admittedly he is a fine boy. But what name would you have chosen if we had kept him?"

"It would have to be Mycroft for sure." We laughed.

# CHAPTER TEN: THE RECKONING

A heavy snowfall greeted us when we awoke the following day, one that completely covered the buildings, trees, and surrounding fields, reminiscent of a winter scene on a Christmas card.

Nicco and Charlotte played outside before breakfast. Wrapped up warmly in winter coats, hats, scarves, gloves and Wellington boots, they pelted each other with snowballs.

Unfortunately the snow didn't start to melt for two days, forcing Libby, her family, and their chauffeur to continue their stay with us. The children loved spending time with their newly acquired aunt and uncle and their cousin Ruben. Then, finally, the servants came back to work, and everything returned to normal. Well, as normal as it gets in the Sapori household.

After breakfast the following day, Sherlock retired to his study to attend to some business matters. He did not join us for luncheon. He finally emerged later in the afternoon to take a shower and change for dinner. It was eight o'clock when we finally sat down to dinner with the children safely ensconced in bed. The house was quiet, save for the chiming of the grandfather clock set in the corner of the room.

Holmes insisted that John Barnaby join us for dinner. So there were five of us settled around the dining table, the room warmed by a crackling log fire.

"Oh, I love your perfume, Nene. It smells familiar. What is it?" quizzed Libby, smiling at me across the table as the starter of oxtail soup was being served.

"It's Mille Fleurs," I replied. "It was a gift from my cousin, Estelle. I've never tried it before, but apparently, it's all the rage back in the States."

The chauffeur, John Barnaby, glanced over towards me. He was a well-built, sallow man with a heavy beard and well-defined eyebrow. I noticed he walked with a slight limp, although without the aid of a stick. John responded to my remarks in a well-modulated voice, his manner gracious and unassuming.

"Ah, Mille Fleurs." He sighed. "It is Georgia's, my dear wife's, favourite. She often wears it. When I smell the aroma, she is in the room with me."

Sherlock studied John intently, running him over with one of his quick, all-comprehensive glances. "Forgive me, John, but from your speech and overall deportment, it's clear you've been educated above your current station. Therefore I deduce that you've served in the military, and an old war wound is undoubtedly the cause of your limp?"

"How on earth could you possibly know that?" asked John, a flabbergasted expression upon his face.

Sherlock chuckled. "It's the way you conduct yourself, John. Your impeccable manners, immaculate uniform and spit-polished boots all give it away. I observed you enter the dining room this evening. You purposely chose a seat facing the door, something a person in the armed forces would be prone to do. I also took the liberty of checking your bedroom earlier today and I must say I was impressed by how neatly you had tucked the sheets under the mattress, as a nurse or someone who had worked in the military would do. Your limp is not recent, for you pay little heed to the affliction, suggesting you were wounded in action. In the Spanish-American War, I would fancy."

John looked at my husband in amazement. "Yes, Mr Holmes, your observations are perfectly accurate. I joined the

First Cavalry Infantry six years ago as a military officer. The conflict was brutal and intense. I was subsequently shot in the thigh by a sniper, hence my injury. But after the atrocities I witnessed, I believe I escaped lightly. However, despite the pain and the bloodshed, we finally won the war when the Spanish surrendered at Santiago on July the seventeenth. I shall never forget that day."

Alun shook his head. "You do yourself a terrible disservice, John. Mr Holmes, this man is a war hero. He was awarded the medal of honour for bravery and promoted to brevet after saving the lives of twenty men from his infantry."

Sherlock pursed his lips, leaning forward in his chair. "Your actions are commendable, John, but pray to tell me what troubles you. For I can tell there is something on your mind of great discomfort."

John responded slowly, pushing his hair back from his head. "Forgive me if I appear distraught, Mr Holmes. My wife and I lost our beloved daughter Yvette only last year—after she committed suicide. Christmas brings back painful memories for me."

John pulled out his handkerchief, wiping a tear from his eye. His pain of mind was heart-rending to observe and affected me profoundly. I recognised the mental anguish of a parent who has suffered the tragic loss of their child. I knew from personal experience that when your child dies, a little bit of you goes with them. The scene reminded me of a phrase from Shakespeare's thirtieth sonnet, which had haunted me from the moment I first read it in school. *Those precious friends hid in death's nameless night.*

John blew his nose before continuing. "When I eventually returned from the Philippines, life was hard for my wife and me. Then I met Mr James, and we soon became friends. He kindly offered me the chauffeur position, and my wife Georgia became the primary housekeeper to the James family." John smiled at Alun. "We have both worked there happily ever since."

Sherlock nodded, appearing satisfied. "I am saddened to hear of your daughter, John. As for your military achievements, they do not surprise me. I can see you are a man of integrity and honour. Please allow me to pour you another drink." He filled up John's glass.

My husband's gaze then moved to his sister. "Libby, you have not been frank with me. But I understand why, and I must give you credit for your loyalty."

Libby stared at her brother nervously before folding her elegant hands in her lap, reminiscent of a chastised child

"Whatever do you mean?" I stared at my husband questioningly.

Sherlock sighed deeply before continuing. "Earlier today, I received a phone call from Inspector Lestrade of the Metropolitan Police. He made inquiries on my behalf with the New York Police Department and the bursar of Trinity School." Libby shifted uncomfortably in her seat, drawing her hands across her temple in an act of profound discomfort.

"What information?" I demanded again.

Sherlock looked at me and grimaced. "There was never a teacher at Trinity named Rick Munroe. Still, a teacher fitting his description left over six months ago, suspected of impropriety with a male pupil, although the school was never able to prove anything. That teacher's name was Beau Adler, the son your uncle adopted."

"Oh my god." I stared at Sherlock, stunned. I then glared at Libby, who'd turned deadly pale. "You must have known all along that Beau was my cousin. Why didn't you say anything?" I was close to tears.

Sherlock shook his head, speaking to me in soft tones. "No, not right away, Nene. But later, when Libby discovered we were married, she would have put two and two together rather quickly. Don't you see? My sister changed Beau's identity to protect you and our family."

"It's true. I swear it, Nene," Libby stared at me anxiously. "We were both duped by Beau. What are the chances?"

"I'm afraid it gets worse," said Sherlock.

"How can it be worse?" I retorted.

Sherlock shook his head gently. "I'm afraid the information I'm about to relay will be somewhat traumatic for both my wife and sister."

"Tell us, please," I pleaded fervently.

"Very well." Sherlock nodded grimly. "Beau Adler was found dead at his apartment in Newark during the Thanksgiving holiday. He shot himself through the temple, leaving behind a suicide note."

Libby and I looked at each other. "Well, I am shocked," I said. "Although Beau never struck me as the suicidal type."

"Indeed." Libby nodded in agreement.

The phone rang. Holmes excused himself before going to his study to answer it.

A sombre mood prevailed as fear heightened suspicion. Alun squeezed Libby's arm. "Are you all right, my dear? This is a dreadful business. I had no time for the fellow, but I would never have wished him dead."

"No, nor I," Libby agreed. She smiled weakly at her husband.

Sherlock entered the room, a serious expression on his face. "That was Lestrade. He received a telegram from the New York Police Department. As I suspected, they were unable to rule out foul play in Beau Adler's death. Indeed, the coroner recorded an open verdict."

I gasped. "Have the police found something suspicious?"

"No, not yet, and I doubt they will," said Sherlock.

"What aren't you telling us?" I quizzed. "What don't the police know?"

After a short pause, Sherlock answered brusquely,

"According to Lestrade, Beau Adler was seated when he allegedly shot himself. And that being the case, it's unlikely his body would have moved from where he sat. This would naturally bring his hand to his side, exactly as the police found him. The gun would have been heavy, so it wouldn't roll or bounce, it would fall onto the floor. Yet the police found the weapon three feet away and on the right-hand side of the body. But even if you consider the weapon's recoil and the type of gun Beau Adler used, a Browning auto-five in this instance, you simply cannot get away from the fact that he was left-handed—as my sister confirmed. Therefore I can only conclude that it would have been a physical impossibility for Beau Adler to have shot himself and end up in that position."

"My God." Libby's fingers gripped the tablecloth. "So you're saying that someone murdered him?"

"Oh, there is no doubt about that," said Sherlock. "Although I would imagine there will be a long list of suspects."

"Yes. Thank goodness Libby was in England at the time," I said.

"Yes, wasn't it?" said Sherlock dryly.

"Do you know who killed him?" I quizzed, staring at Sherlock curiously.

"Yes, of course, Nene. It's a simple matter," Sherlock rejoined abruptly. "The person who witnessed the crime is sitting here with us in this room." Sherlock arched an eyebrow. His face tightened as his attention diverted to Alun.

"You cannot be serious if you think I was responsible." Alun's eyes narrowed, shaking his head in disbelief.

"Why not?" said Sherlock, a faint irony in his voice. "A man generally protests upon discovering his wife has been impregnated by her lover. The same man who, in an act of spite and vindictiveness, sent you compromising pictures of her through the post."

"You go too far, Holmes," cried Alun. He glanced across at

Libby, who looked horrified.

"I'm sorry, Alun," said Libby, tears rolling down her face. "It was a moment of madness, and I couldn't bring myself to tell you."

Alan nodded. "It's all right, Lib. I forgive you. And I swear to god that I did *not* kill that man."

Sherlock' face retained a state of intense concentration. "My sister said she was in England at the time of Adler's death, but we only have her word for that." Sherlock sighed deeply. "Everyone sitting around this table had a motive for killing Beau Adler, including my wife and me. I've been trying to find a way to bring Adler to justice for years for a crime he committed years ago. As for my wife, she was on stage at La Scala on the night in question."

I smiled at my husband, shaking my head. "Oh, believe me, if I'd wanted to kill my cousin, I would have done it before now."

Sherlock nodded. "That man touched all our lives in one way or another. Including you, John."

John looked at Sherlock in amazement, bowing his head in acquiescence. "Yes, you are right, of course, Mr Holmes. I freely admit it was me who killed Adler."

Sherlock shook his head. "I know you didn't fire the gun, John. Although, ultimately, you are indirectly responsible for that man's death. Your daughter's suicide — I fancy something happened between her and Adler. Something so dreadful that it caused her to take her own life. But it was a woman who entered Beau Adler's apartment and fired the gun. When the police discovered the body, they reported a lingering smell of Mille Fleur's perfume. The police put it down to an ex-lover hell-bent on revenge. But they're wrong. A lover would have had an intimate knowledge of their partner. They would have known Beau Adler was left-handed. No, it could only be the woman you are screening, John . . .your wife."

John began to sob softly. He eventually responded in a low voice, speaking with an intensity that silenced the room. "Yes, Mr Holmes. This isn't easy for me to relay. You have no idea what my wife and I endured at the hands of that man. In the autumn of last year, our beloved daughter Yvette moved to Newark to take up a position as governess to the Upton family in Forest Hill. Unfortunately, she met Adler and became besotted with him. She'd always been a headstrong girl. Everything seemed fine for a while until Adler threw her over for another woman. But unfortunately, that wasn't the affair's end. Adler kept coming back to torment Yvette. It completely broke her heart. The last time my wife and I saw Yvette alive, we could see livid bruises all over her face and body.

"But when we confronted her, she denied everything. We were naturally concerned for her well-being. Our daughter confided to us that her lover kept a gun under the window seat in the hallway, hidden inside the sleeve of a book that had been hollowed out. Eventually I went to see him. I pleaded with him to let my daughter be. But he laughed in my face and told me he would do what he wanted. After that the abuse got far worse, something I've always reproached myself for. Our daughter left a note saying she couldn't go on. She was twenty-five . . .bright, beautiful, with the world at her feet. So I beg of you Mr Holmes, please don't punish my wife. She's been through enough already. I'll tell the police it was me who committed the crime."

Sherlock leaned forward in his chair. He stared at John with a look of intense concentration. "I know what Adler did was terrible—he was a despicable man. Pray, tell me, John, what compelled your wife to carry out such a heinous crime?"

John took a deep breath. "When my daughter died, my wife and I called on Beau Adler to tell him the devastating news and to collect some of Yvette's belongings. He appeared shocked and visibly upset at first and invited us into his apartment. When we looked around, it was apparent he had another woman there. When we confronted Adler, his mood changed. He called our daughter a whore, and other shocking profanities that I couldn't possibly repeat in front of the ladies. Georgia and I were devastated and stormed out of the apartment." John glanced over towards Libby. "I believe it's fair to say that Mrs James is exceptionally close to my wife."

Libby nodded. "Yes, that's right," she agreed. "Georgia has always been like a mother to me. I could tell her anything. Although I wish she'd confided in me about Yvette."

John shook his head. "Georgia wanted to tell you, Mrs James, but in the end she thought you had more than enough to deal with. She knew you and Mr James were not getting on at the time and she would have had no way of knowing about the connection between you and our daughter."

Libby nodded. "I remember breaking down in front of Georgia in August before I came to London. And I eventually confided in her all that had transpired in Manhattan, including my pregnancy and the impending adoption."

John smiled at Libby gently. "You must surely remember, Mrs James, that photograph with the alumni of teachers from Trinity school. The one you kept in your bedroom drawer? One day in late November, my wife was cleaning your room. She wanted everything to be spick and span in anticipation of your return. And it was there Georgia discovered the photograph. She was shocked to see Beau Adler staring back at her, a smug expression upon his face. He was standing next to you in the photograph, Mrs James. Georgia's blood ran cold, and you can imagine her horror when she realised it was Adler who had been your lover and was the father of your unborn child. When Georgia came home and told me, I was stunned. I couldn't believe Mr James had been cuckolded by the man responsible for our daughter's death."

John sighed and stared hard at my husband. "Take it from

me, Mr Holmes, your sister and her child had a most fortunate escape. My wife was inconsolable. She adores your sister — she loves her like a daughter. Then Georgia became angry. "How many more lives is this man going to destroy before someone stops him," she said. She was determined to confront Adler again and I reluctantly agreed to accompany her.

"When we arrived at Adler's apartment on Thanksgiving Day, it was almost dusk. Adler reluctantly let us in, a twisted smirk on his features. He invited us to sit, and he took a seat in his armchair. My wife asked to use the bathroom and he agreed, waving his hand dismissively. Then I confronted Adler about how he'd treated your sister, Mr Holmes. Well, he looked astounded and asked how I knew, so I told him that I worked for Mr James. Adler then became animated and told us he should have shut Libby James up while he had the chance. He said it would not be the first time he'd disposed of someone, and if my wife and I dared to meddle in his affairs again he would come after Georgia and Mrs James. My wife was crying, at this point, hysterical — she reached into her coat pocket and revealed the gun she'd removed from the window seat in the hallway. She pointed it at Adler, but she couldn't bring herself to pull the trigger, Mr Holmes."

John paused and took a sip from his glass before continuing. "Adler made a lunge for the gun. It went off by accident, shooting him straight through the temple. We quickly realised he was dead and there was nothing to be done. So I put him back into his chair, my wife placed the gun at the side of the body and quickly wrote out a suicide note. Georgia is skilled in calligraphy. She copied out Adler's signature from a letter we found on his desk. I know I will probably swing for what happened, but I have no remorse for that monster's demise. Although I will be sorry to leave my wife. She will now be alone in the world. Yvette was our only child." He sighed. "Now you know everything. So do your worst, Mr

Holmes, for I am prepared for the consequences."

Sherlock did not appear in the least bit surprised by John's narrative. "This is a perplexing business. I need to give it careful consideration before I reach a definite conclusion. I suggest we all retire for the night. I will let you have my decision in the morning. I take it, as an officer and a gentleman, I can trust you not to make a run for it, John?"

John shook his head. "I am a man of honour, Mr Holmes, as you rightly pointed out. You have my word that I will remain in this house until you have reached your decision."

The guests quietly departed and made their way upstairs, leaving Sherlock and me alone in the dining room. After a short pause, Sherlock quietly said, "Would you like to take a little whiskey, as I think we should?" I nodded in agreement.

Sherlock smiled at me grimly. His hand gently squeezed my arm to comfort me before leaving the room. He returned with a silver tray containing a decanter, siphon, and two crystal glasses. Sherlock poured out the whiskey. I declined the soda before he handed one to me. I sipped from it slowly, savouring the bitter taste of the amber liquid, staring at him with a perplexed expression.

"Well," I said. "Surely you cannot even consider reporting John to the police? What that poor man and his wife endured is indescribable. Your sister and nephew are fortunate to have escaped with their lives."

Sherlock shook his head. "You know I must, Nene. Murder is a capital offence. I simply cannot ignore that John was responsible for a man's death—even if that man was the devil incarnate."

"And what if it had been Charlotte? Or me? What then? Would you still feel the same? To appreciate what that man has gone through, as a father and a husband, you need to walk in his shoes."

"Why, if he laid a hand on either you or the children, I

would want to kill him. But, if I was faced with that person, I'd like to think I could find the strength to do the right thing." Sherlock stared at me with a brooding intensity. "And it was nearly you, Nene, all those years ago. When you were fifteen. It still makes me shudder to even think of that moral turpitude. What that paedophile tried to do to an innocent child. I shall sleep on it tonight. Things will become more evident in the morning, of that I have no doubt."

Everyone was seated around the breakfast table by the strike of nine the following morning.

Sherlock sipped from his coffee cup, the gravest of expressions upon his face. He leaned back in his chair, staring out the window for a moment, his attention clearly distracted by the sound of the children's laughter as they played outside in the melting snow.

All eyes in the room fixed upon him expectantly. Finally, he laid down his coffee cup. He put his fingers together and leaned his elbows on his chair to address his captive audience.

"I intend to speak to Inspector Lestrade later this morning," said Sherlock. There was a collective gasp echoing around the room as Sherlock continued. "I shall inform him that I will no longer be pursuing my enquiries about Beau Adler's death." Sherlock smiled at John. "I believe you and your family have suffered enough, so you are free, John. Go home and take care of your wife. Please convey to her my sincerest regards."

John stared at Sherlock incredulously. My husband's narrative had sparked a glimmer of life back into his sallow cheeks. "Thank you, Mr Holmes, from the bottom of my heart. My wife and I will be forever indebted to you."

"No need." Sherlock concluded by holding up his hand, his own face flushed with colour. "You will forgive me if I retire to my study. I have a few phone calls to make and some small businesses to attend to. I look forward to seeing you all this evening for our last supper. I have no doubt you will be planning to travel on the morrow. Perhaps, if we ask nicely, my wife might sing?"

"Yes, of course. It would be my absolute pleasure. Music is such a great therapy." I beamed at my husband.

Later that morning, I entered the study to find Sherlock seated at his desk covered with scribbled papers and notes, flanked by a glass of whiskey and an overflowing ashtray. Setting a cup of coffee down, within his reach, I smiled at my husband.

"I'm glad you came to that decision. I appreciate that it could not have been easy. I'm so proud of you,".

He nodded. "Indeed, it was a difficult decision morally, but I believe the correct one in the end. I took heed of what you said, Nene, and considered all the facts laid before me as a father, husband, brother, and detective. Perhaps if I'd remained a bachelor, I might have come to a different conclusion. But at least my family is safe. That's all that matters. I had no idea that the peculiarity and complexity of this case would prove to be like my wife . . . irresistible." He drew me to him and kissed me gently on the lips.

Libby and her family finally left us on Thursday, December the twenty-ninth. John brought the car to the front of the house, and I carefully handed the baby to his mother.

"The next time you're in New Jersey, promise you'll come and see us. You're the closest thing I have to a sister." Libby embraced me warmly before putting on her gloves and wrapping a cashmere scarf around her neck.

"Yes, we will try," I promised.

Libby's dulcet toned voice called out to her brother. "Your wife and children are remarkable. At least we now know who the true genius in our family is. I'll give you a clue. As clever as he thinks he is, it's not our brother."

"What do you mean?" Sherlock stared at his sister with a bemused expression.

"You, brother, are a legend, my brilliant nephew Nicco is as bright as a button, but the lovely Charlotte will always be the superior intellect. You mark my words, that child will go far."

Sherlock shrugged. "You may well have a point. Admittedly, Charlotte is far more intelligent than you at her age."

We waved goodbye to Libby and Alun. Before the car disappeared from view, Libby turned round in her seat and smiled at me, the strangest expression on her face. The words she uttered to me in the birthing room rang in my ears. *I would be prepared to do anything for my brother.* As I had no doubt Georgia would be prepared to do anything for Libby.

"Never mind, Charlotte." Nicco placed a comforting arm around his sister's shoulder. "You never know, another baby may arrive before next Christmas."

"Is there something I should know?" Sherlock stared at me in mock amusement.

"No." I shook my head. "I'm sorry, children. I'm afraid the stork has made his final visit to Ash Tree Farm. But we have a puppy, a yearling, and two nanny goats to dote on. We should be grateful for that." I took the children by the hand. "Let's get you inside for hot chocolate and cake." I glanced at Sherlock. "Will you take me into town later? I need a rug for Shadow."

Sherlock nodded. "Yes, of course." He glanced at his watch chain. "Give me an hour or so, as I expect a phone call. Ah, here it is now," he said as the phone rang. He dashed inside to answer it.

I took the children into the kitchen where I left them drinking hot chocolate and eating cake in our housemaid Mary's more than capable hands.

Half an hour later, Sherlock came into the drawing room to announce he'd brought the brougham round to the side of the house.

"Are you all right, Nene?" he asked.

"Yes, I'm fine. It's all been a shock, but at least your sister gets her happy ending. Beau will never hurt anyone again. First, however, I should go and see my relatives in the Catskills and extend my condolences. Of course my father would have expected it of me. But, given our history, it's not a journey I wish to take alone." I gazed at my husband expectantly.

He smiled at me, a glint in his eyes. "I could never allow you to travel alone under such circumstances. I am your husband, it's my duty to protect you. Naturally I shall accompany you. It's always a joy to meet an American, so I shall look forward to meeting your relatives. We can visit New York simultaneously and check out Broadway, your old haunting ground." Holmes paused for a moment, a mischievous look in his eye. "But, if we are to travel together, I have two conditions."

"Fine." I immediately replied.

"You don't yet know what they are?" He chuckled at my response.

"First, I shall call Mrs Hudson and ask her to look after the children. The servants would undoubtedly manage, but I will feel happier knowing that Nicco and Charlotte are under Mrs Hudson's care. Then I will ask Mycroft to instruct his security guard, Albert, to drive Mrs Hudson here tomorrow and remain at Ash Tree Farm until we return."

"And what is the second condition?" I stared at him curiously.

"Why, that we travel in disguise and incognito, of course. As Mr and Mrs Sigerson. What do you say, Nene? Are you up to the challenge?"

"Absolutely," I cried, thrilled at the idea of travelling to New York and spending quality time with my husband. "But I have a condition of my own."

Sherlock looked at me with a flicker of amusement in his grey astute eyes. "You know I could never deny you anything you asked of me, Nene."

"Except perhaps another child?"

He shook his head. "But then you already know the reasons for that. After what happened with Charlotte, I couldn't bear the thought of losing you."

I sighed. "Yes, I understand, no more babies. You're right, of course. We have already done splendidly for Queen and country. We are fortunate indeed to have two such remarkable children. Perhaps now might be time for us to have some new adventures. What do you say, Mr Holmes?"

"A capital idea." He laughed at my parting shot. "Let's hope we don't encounter another Moriarty sibling along the way. But you haven't yet told me your condition?"

"When we return here, I plan to take the children to Milan. I'd like you to come with us." I gazed into his eyes. "And then I want to go back to Fiesole."

Sherlock hesitated for a moment, then smiled. "Then I shall make arrangements forthwith. Give me ten minutes, Nene, and then we'll head into town and see what it has to offer the likes of you and me."

# Epilogue: Letting Go

To love a genius is a special thing. For when he appears before you, and you come to know him, you will realise that he is a form of wonder to behold – Irene Adler.

It was a cold crisp day, the sun hidden behind a cloudless sky, as Sherlock and I disembarked from our transatlantic voyage from Southampton to the port of New York. We had messaged ahead to my uncle, Aloysius, who we found waiting patiently in his car, puffing away on a cigarette. Although I hadn't seen him for years, I immediately recognised the tall, slim, imposing figure in a black sack suit. The intense blue sparkling eyes covered with half-moon spectacles reminded me of my late father. His once jet-black hair, now bespeckled grey, was concealed under a billycock hat. I introduced my uncle to my husband before collapsing into my uncle's arms, crying out with joy and relief.

We set off on our journey, making our way to Livingston Manor, located to the South of Rockland. Aloysius pointed out places of interest I was familiar with, such as Beaverkill Bridge and Sonoma Falls, where my uncle took my cousins and me fishing in the summer. Sherlock sat quietly for much of the journey, staring in awe at the stunning scenery. Like me, I could tell he was impressed by the breath-taking beauty of the mountains where I played and ran freely as a child.

When we arrived at the ranch, Columbine Valley Farm, we were greeted warmly by my cousins Denis, Desmond, and their wives and children, who were all delightful. Desmond's wife Melanie cooked us a splendid dinner of lentil and mushroom pate, whole grilled trout (the official fish of the Catskills), served with tamari sauce, rice, and green beans, and then my favourite olive cake for dessert. All washed down with copious amounts of fine wine and Kentucky bourbon.

I looked around the table at the beaming faces of my family. My heart warmed to see my husband making an effort to interact with them. I knew then that despite all the anguish and pain I'd endured, in the end it mattered not because everything was going to work out fine.

After dinner, Sherlock and my uncle retired to the lounge for cigars and brandy. I took the opportunity to explore the stable block with my cousins and look at the quarter horses. I could feel Beau's presence. But I was no longer afraid. Thanks to my husband, I could finally lay my demons to rest.

As for my Aunt Susannah, she never returned to the ranch. After she and Aloysius officially separated, she moved to Baltimore to live with her sister. I finally reassured my uncle that there was nothing to forgive after explaining how I was betrayed and badly let down by my Aunt Susannah, who had chosen Beau and his dreadful secret over the rest of her family by keeping Aloysius and my cousins in the dark for years. My uncle was delighted when I agreed to his request to bring the children to the Catskills in the summer holidays.

The following morning, after a leisurely breakfast. Sherlock and I bid my family a fond farewell and Denis drove us to the railway station, where we caught the train to Grand Central in New York, finally arriving at our hotel in Times Square. I revelled in showing my bemused husband the sights and sounds of Manhattan. However, he stubbornly refused to get on any of the sightseeing buses, preferring to use the electric hansom cabs that thronged the streets. We took in an outstanding production of Puccini's dramatic opera *Tosca* on

Broadway. I remember Sherlock squeezing my hand to console me when I wept uncontrollably as Tosca clasped Cavaradossi's lifeless body.

The day before our ship set sail for Southampton, we met up with Libby, Alun, and Estelle at Faunce, where Alun gave us a fine luncheon. We spent a wonderful afternoon together, making merry with wine and cocktails and catching up on our news.

We arrived back at Ash Tree Farm only to discover Sherlock had a crucial case demanding his attention at Baker Street. So it was agreed that I would take the children back to Milan. I somehow managed to conceal my disappointment, grateful for our time together in America.

So you can imagine my delight when Sherlock unexpectedly arrived in Milan four weeks later to announce he would accompany me to Fiesole. When I questioned my husband, he said he felt compelled to take me. He understood how much it meant to me, to both of us. So we spent a magical week with our friends Ludo and Violetta, and despite their protests, Sherlock and I insisted on staying in the barn, where we'd fallen in love all those years ago. Those few weeks were among some of the happiest moments of my life.

When I returned to Milan, I felt like a new woman, invigorated from spending time with the man I loved and friends and relatives I adored. I decided that I was more than ready for any new adventures that were to come. Little did I know then that there would be many.

The End

# ABOUT THE AUTHOR

KD Sherrinford was born and raised in Preston, Lancashire, and now resides on The Fylde Coast with her husband John, and their four children. An avid reader from an early age, KD was fascinated by the stories of Sir Arthur Conan Doyle and Agatha Christie, she read the entire Doyle Canon by the time she was 13. A talented pianist, KD played piano from age six, the music of some of her favourite composers, Beethoven, Schubert, Stephen Foster, and Richard Wagner, all strongly feature in her books. KD had a varied early career, working with thoroughbred horses, and racing greyhounds, she and her husband won the Blackpool Greyhound Derby in 1987 with Scottie. Then to mix things up KD joined Countrywide, where she was employed for over 20 years and became a Fellow of The National Association of Estate Agents. Retirement finally gave KD the opportunity to follow her dreams and start work on her first novel. She gained inspiration to write" Song for Someone" from her daughter Katie, after a visit to the Sherlock Holmes museum on Baker Street in 2019. It had always been a passion to write about Irene Adler, she is such an iconic character, and KD wanted to give her a voice. KD recently completed her second book in the Sherlock Holmes and Irene Adler mystery series, "Christmas at The Sapori's", and is currently working on the third book in the series "Meet me in Milan."

KD Sherrinford can be found on her author page: https://www.facebook.com/people/KD-Sherrinford-100078319333010

To find out the latest email: kdsherrinford@gmail.com or check out the website: www.kdsherrinford.co.uk